Dragon Run

Dragon Run

by CARLEY DAWSON

Illustrated by LYND WARD

1955

HOUGHTON MIFFLIN COMPANY

The Riverside Press Cambridge

To

Three very different C's

L. H.

M. K.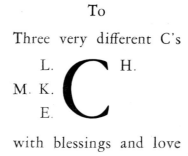

E.

with blessings and love

C.

CHAPTER 1

*O*N A FINE SEPTEMBER day, Chris Mason, four-- teen, with his parents, drove through the streets of Washington, D.C. They had just locked the door of their Georgetown house behind them, and were now driving through the streets of the oldest part of the capital city. Fall had come early. The maple trees, whose roots humped the worn brick pavements of Georgetown, made a sunlight of their own before the doors of the brick or clapboard houses that faced the quiet roads.

Chris, in the back seat, mused as they drove out of town. He had agreed to go with his father and mother for a special purpose: house-hunting. For some months they had been talking of what fun it would be to have a small house in the country. A flower garden for Mrs. Mason; a small vegetable garden for Chris and his father to putter in. There would be the joy of seeing acres of sky, and the slow impressive wheel of the seasons. They had discussed, evening after evening, how it would be — a blazing fire in the fireplace of their living room on winter days; supper outside on a terrace on hot summer nights, where the fireflies winked over the lawn and tangled in the flowers. Earlier on that particular Saturday morning, when the sun seemed to reflect a sheen of lemon and apricot from the maple leaves, Commander Mason had thrown open the door of Chris's bedroom.

"Hit the deck, boy! This is the day we find our house. Your mother's putting up a lunch — half an hour and we're off. Rise and shine!"

Chris, galvanized by his father's tone and the brilliance of the day, swung his legs out of bed. As usual, the first thing his eyes saw was his prize possession, given to him as a memento of a never-to-be-forgotten adventure a year before. Then, only a boy of thirteen, he had ventured into the shop of an old antiquarian, Mr. Wicker, and had from that moment begun a fantastic series of events that even now seemed hard to believe.

Chris smiled at the model of a ship in a bottle, the *Mirabelle*, and getting dressed, did not forget to put his lucky piece, an old Spanish coin, into his pocket. This was a reminder of a second voyage, also on the *Mirabelle*, with his friend the extraordinary Mr. Wicker. Mr. Wicker, Chris alone knew, was a magician without peer, and with only one deadly and dangerous rival.

A frown crossed Chris's young face as the picture of Mr. Wicker's enemy rose before him. Pirate though he was, Claggett Chew was also a magician, second only to Mr. Wicker. The cold face, the icy eyes peering brutally from under the crags of bushy eyebrows; the shaven head; the strong hands grasping the poison-tipped leather whip — no wonder that Chris gave an involuntary shudder whenever he thought of this man.

Still, he missed his friends who lived in the past, in the eighteenth century, which twice, now, he had been able to re-enter. It was through his own ability, a rare gift, of being able to move backward and forward in Time itself that Chris could, at long intervals, leave his own century and go back into the 1790's. There many of his closest friends were living their lives, unaware of the power of their friend Chris, or that of their master William Wicker, merchant and magician.

Becky Boozer was there, in 1795, in the neat brick house near the eighteenth-century port of Georgetown as Mr. Wicker's imposing housekeeper, six feet tall and brawnily buxom, moving under the permanent shadow of her vast bonnet. Chris could never think of Becky and her hat without laughing — the hat the poor soul had saved for so long to buy, proud of its twenty-four roses and twelve waving black plumes. This fabulous bonnet was at all times on her head, some said, because the Devil himself had caused it to be a permanent fixture.

There, too, was Becky's steadfast admirer, Ned Cilley, the bandy-legged sailor, tousled of sand-colored head and with hit-or-miss teeth in a mouth perpetually stretched in a friendly grin. I wonder, Chris thought to himself, if Ned's appetite is as insatiable as ever — while saying that he can't eat a crumb or a morsel!

Thinking of his friends, Chris began to long for a sight of his companion in adventure, dark-skinned Amos. Amos, he reflected, must be tall and strong now, for although Amos was of an age with Chris he had always shown signs of being taller and more muscular.

A shout up the stairwell roused Chris from his daydreaming.

"Hey, sailor! Are you lost in that crow's-nest of yours? The galley's about to close for the day!"

Chris hurried down the stairs, gulped his breakfast, and the Mason family were off.

Commander Mason turned the car into Wisconsin Avenue from O Street, and as they reached the traffic light at M, Chris craned his neck toward the distant corner of Wisconsin and Water Streets. He knew only too well that he could not see his friends in the past that day, yet the glimpse he had of the antiquarian's shop where in the twentieth century Mr. Wicker sold antiques was somehow satisfying. Chris knew the house and shop so well, the low brick house with its verge of grass,

4

its border of flowers and shrubs near the busy street, the hidden garden behind sheltered by trees and a high wall, that he really had no need of the quick glance he took as the car turned right along M, heading for the Chain Bridge.

"Looking for old Wicker?" his father asked Chris over his shoulder.

"Mm-mm," Chris murmured.

Chris's mother broke in. "He's nice, Mr. Wicker. I like him." She was smiling a reminiscent smile. "His face is unbelievably wrinkled and old — I declare, he might be one hundred. Except for his eyes."

"Eyes?" queried her husband, his own watching the traffic.

"Yes," Mrs. Mason went on, "his eyes are quite eerie. They're not old at all. In fact — " she laughed a little self-consciously and turned her head just enough to give a side look at her husband, " — his eyes give the impression of belonging to a young, and — yes — a very attractive man."

"Come, come, my dear," the Commander chided, "no wonder Chris is fanciful sometimes. I can see where it comes from. Attractive? Old Wicker!"

"Well — he was young once," she persisted, "that's certain. And somehow, his eyes have remained so. He gave me a look that — "

"Yes?" her husband inquired drily.

Mrs. Mason gave another short laugh. "Well, had he been younger, it would have been almost flirtatious. But not his manner. Don't misunderstand me. He has beautiful old-fashioned manners." She gave the trace of a sigh. "It was only a hint in his eyes."

Chris nearly laughed aloud. For he knew, as perhaps no other person in the present day did, that Mr. Wicker could change back from his wizened, ancient appearance of the twentieth century to a man in the prime of life. Then he would be ruddy-skinned, with dark chestnut hair caught at the back of his head with a sober black bow, and strong white teeth under a straight aristocratic nose. His eyes, as Mrs. Mason remarked, appreciated a pretty woman. Intelligent and brooding, they could also spark with quick humor.

Chris abandoned remembrances to find that they had left

6

the rocky, dashing Potomac and were on the main highway leading to Leesburg, Virginia. His father was speaking.

"We haven't investigated that narrow panhandle of West Virginia that used to be a part of Virginia until the Civil War. There should be some good houses along there. It was frontier country — families moved up from the settlements of the James River; the first large house built around there was Harewood, I believe, in 1750. Right, Chris?"

"Yes sir, I think so."

"Hump! Don't seem too sure. A lot of good school does! Here we are at Leesburg."

They drove through the quaint town; the courthouse set back from the road among trees, the streets narrow and not meant for steady mechanized traffic. Outside Leesburg, a few miles farther on, the road dipped to the right, and far ahead lay a graceful line of blue hills.

"There are the Blue Ridge mountains!" Commander Mason exclaimed. "On the other side lies West Virginia, and perhaps — who knows? — a small house meant for the Masons. How about it, Chris?"

Chris felt an inner excitement such as had not touched him for many a day. He leaned forward, his eyes on the approaching blue hills rising above rolling fields.

"Yes, sir!" he answered, his tone vigorous. "I have a feeling this might be our lucky day."

"So do I!" his mother and father replied simultaneously.

7

CHAPTER 2

HE FARMS OF THE country near the Blue Ridge seemed isolated, such was the spread of their fields. The Masons drove through Hillsboro, with its gray fieldstone meetinghouse standing on a knoll in an oak grove. Disappearing behind them the signpost pointed to Harper's Ferry on their right as they drove up the steep slope of the Blue Ridge hills.

The Blue Ridge was only blue at a distance. Autumn had touched the trees with its own magic, and chrome yellow, flame, rust red, the massed trees swept up the hillsides like a forest fire. At the top of the ridge a road sign announced the dividing line between the two states, adding a welcome from Jefferson County, West Virginia. The road ran along the ridgetop, and as it shot down the other side, a breath-taking view was disclosed. All three Masons sat forward. Chris's father stopped the car and they got out to see the miles of country far below.

The mountain dropped sharply at their feet, and at its base, the broad silver band of the Shenandoah river made a giant horseshoe bend. Pastures and woods edged the water. Cliffs and bluffs, undulating fields of green, yellow or the red of Virginia soil, bordered the river that glittered where limestone ledges broke the water into shoals. Small homesteads stood out like miniature fortresses among the acres of wild land, and beyond lay the plains on the other side of Charles Town. Farther still, wavered the distant horizon of yet another line of mountains.

"What this must be in the spring!" Mrs. Mason exclaimed, after a long look in every direction. "This is apple country, Chris. There are miles of apple orchards all around that will be white with blossom in the spring, like a late snowfall."

The Commander was gazing down at the river. "I understand there's good bass fishing in the Shenandoah," he murmured. Then, looking up and swinging his arms wide, "That's fine country to be a part of!" he cried.

Chris, looking at the land that reached as far as the eye could see, and at the sinuous winding river, felt the nudge of adventure at his elbow.

A steel bridge crossed the Shenandoah at the foot of the mountain. The river wandered past the forested crags with not a house to be seen on the high mountainside. It was not hard for Chris to picture the deer, raccoon, and 'possum that must have their hidden trails along the cliffs. Or imagine the Indians who had once hunted there, later to terrify the first settlers, and drive away bands of the women and children who had been hardy enough to penetrate, with their husbands and fathers, into the then uncharted country.

Once across the steel bridge, they came to the town of Bloomery.

9

"What a strange name," Mrs. Mason said.

"I believe this is the site of one of the country's first iron-works, or iron foundry, or bloomery," Chris's father replied. "George Washington visited the foundry when he was a young man, and it may have been then that he bought the land nearby where his brother, Charles, built his fine house, Happy Retreat. The house is still there. Charles Town was named after Charles Washington, you know. Perhaps we'll see the house later on. But," he continued, as the car moved up the hill beside a house of squared logs, "there's a lane — just a country road — leading off to the left up here, that I saw once. I've had a hankering to follow it."

They turned left at the top of the hill. Ahead, on the right, a white farmhouse was backed by a red-painted barn of tremendous size. Another farmhouse with pillared porch lay to the left, and the road dipped suddenly toward a narrow bridge.

Beside a stream in a little vale stood a dilapidated house of vertical clapboard. A huge fieldstone chimney rose up at one side, and a wide fireplace with a smaller one above showed that at some time another building had made an angle, or wing, to the block of the main house. The size of the chimney and lower fireplace seemed out of proportion with what remained of the house. With one accord three pairs of eyes were riveted on the little white building with the formidable chimney. Commander Mason slowed the car as they all stared at it. It seemed to stare back, singularly self-possessed in spite of its decrepitude. Behind it rose the pale yellow of willows with a distant field beyond.

"What's that?" Chris was the first to ask.

10

"I *like* that house!" his mother exclaimed.

"Let's have a look," said the Commander, and the car rolled forward across the bridge.

A roar came through the open windows of the car, and looking through the turning leaves, the Masons caught sight of a thirty-foot waterfall, flashing white into a pool below. A stream surrounded the house and the trees bordering it stood tall and thick, of great age.

"Can we go in, do you think?" Chris asked. "It doesn't seem to be lived in — "

"It *does* seem vacant. No harm in trying," his father answered.

The three Washingtonians stood beside their car for a moment, looking down the rough grass lawn past a mighty sycamore to the house with the big chimney.

The bright day was clouding over, and the sun was hidden. A deep shadow swept over the pasture behind the house, and a sinister look touched even the surrounding trees. A shaft of light pierced the cloud, jabbing the windowpanes with instant fire as if someone inside the house had lit a candle or a lamp. The waterfall, only a moment before glittering blue over the rocky shelf, was abruptly leaden and cold. A hiss of wind like a snake wound through the trees and the light in the windows was quenched, as though the lamp had been overthrown.

"Funny," the Commander said, his voice troubled. "It looks quite different now. I thought I saw — "

"I don't like it any more," Mrs. Mason added slowly. "It isn't really as cheerful as I had thought at first — "

"Isn't it sort of cold here?" Chris ventured. "How about driving down the road a way?"

They were quiet getting back into the car. There was a keen disappointment on every face, each one trying to recapture what he had fancied they had seen so clearly before they crossed the bridge.

"Let's go a little farther down," Mrs. Mason encouraged. "I'm hungry. Let's find a nice place for lunch."

They found a good rise of ground from where the Blue Ridge stood close above them with rolling fields between. The river was lost to view under the mountainside; far away they could see the warm red of a large brick house. They admired

12

its symmetry and location as they ate their sandwiches and hard-boiled eggs.

"Looks like an old plantation restored," Mrs. Mason said, biting into an apple. "If we see anyone, let's ask."

"And about the house with the waterfall," Chris added, chewing.

"Here comes someone down the road, now," Commander Mason said, and got up to hail the passer-by.

It was a farmer on a tractor, rattling down the narrow lane. He stopped at Commander Mason's raised hand and friendly smile.

"We won't keep you but a moment," Commander Mason began. "We're investigating this fine part of the country, and were wondering about that house down there." He pointed to the red brick building, its solid square center flanked by long arched wings on either side, with a smaller square house at each end. The farmer twisted about in his seat to look, as if he had never seen it before instead of having been familiar with it since his childhood, and knowing it had stood there since his grandfather's time.

"Oh — Riveridge," he said. "You don't know Riveridge?" His face was incredulous. "It's open to the public during Garden Week — been put in good shape by the new owners."

"New owners?" prompted the Commander.

"Yes. Used to be owned by the Moffit family for generations — them and their descendants — and then stood vacant fifteen or twenty years." He looked back over his shoulder at the house with a touch of affection in his face. "Bought by northerners five years ago. Seem like nice enough folks. They've spent a packet on the place. Put back the gardens and all, just

13

like they was. Or so the old folks hereabouts say."

Chris had come forward quickly as the farmer had begun to speak. "Who did you say had owned it?" he asked breathlessly, his eyes lifted to the weather-beaten face above him.

The man looked down. "Moffit," he said. "The place was famous in its time. Way back, old lady Moffit was quite a character. Sort of a legend round about here. Or so they tell —"

"Did she have a granddaughter named Susan?" Chris asked, the pink of rising excitement beginning to show in his cheeks.

The farmer looked at him without change of expression.

"Might've. Had a separate, smaller plantation relations lived in, mile or two further on. All the same land. Or was then."

Mrs. Mason came up in her turn. "What *is* the little house with the waterfall?" she asked, pointing back the way they had come. "Who owns it?"

The farmer shook his head. " 'Tain't owned by anybody much, I guess. Place is pretty run down. Never was anything but a ol' log house with clapboard. Logs underneath is still good, I guess. All the houses round about here is of logs, just about. Excepting Riveridge."

"Who *did* own the place?" Chris persisted, only now dimly beginning to understand why he had to know.

The farmer was beginning to get impatient at so many questions.

"First off, man by the name of Chew," he said scratching his head. "Way back, that was. Queer stories about the man. No one knows the straight of it now, I reckon, but seems like he was a prettty bad character. Since, it's passed through several hands — "

"Thanks," Chris said, in a daze. Chew! he thought. There could be only one. "What's the name of the stream that makes the waterfall?" he inquired.

"Dragon Run," the man said flatly, started up the tractor, waved his hand and rattled off.

Chris knew then that on the very next day he must revisit his old friends, Mr. Wicker, Becky, and Amos.

15

CHAPTER 3

*T*HE SERMON SEEMED unending to Chris that Sunday morning. He had his parents' permission to visit Mr. Wicker immediately after church, and his thoughts were more often outside the brick church at 31st and O Streets than inside it.

When at last he could dash around the corner and start off at a lope down the hill past the post office, he felt that he had already seen Mr. Wicker and wished him a boisterous good morning, so often had he made the journey in his mind.

As always, the September sun shattered into blue and gold fragments what little could be seen of the Potomac between the smokestacks and walls of the river-edging factories. Chris's impatience was slowed when he could see below him the loved brick walls and familiar roof of the antiquarian's house. Once again, he could not keep back a shiver as he wondered whether the fragile Mr. Wicker of the twentieth century was still in good health and able to receive him. Whether his old friends were still in the big kitchen whose twin windows gave on to

Water Street, with its view of ships and the port? Whether Amos still slept upstairs, over the kitchen in the attic, in the neat bedroom with the mansard windows that had once been his? And if, indeed, a year's growth had interfered with his own ability to go back into that pleasant time? As he neared the well-known bow window and white-painted door, the same fear he always had assailed him — that all those who were so dear to his heart might have vanished beyond his power to regain them. The boy's face was white and tense with anxiety when he stood hesitant in front of the house and the Time he longed to re-enter.

He gave a glance to the right, to the rumbling of cars on the overhead traffic lane; frowned at how completely the ugly factories cut off the sweep of the river below Key Bridge, and setting his teeth against his terror that all might be changed, flung open the door under the worn sign:

W<small>LLM.</small> WICKER, CURIOSITIES.

The bell jangled and fell silent. Chris stood in the empty shop, feeling his knees weaken and his teeth chatter with nerves. No footstep came to him of his ancient friend, and after a long moment he turned in despair to leave, his eyes half blinded by tears of grief and desolation.

As he faced about, the bow window with its dusty assortment of odds and ends confronted him, and swimming blurrily into his sight swept the calm, clear Georgetown of 1795. Gone were the factories and the overhead traffic route; a peaceable silence engulfed him. The two warehouses across the way, falling into disrepair in his own time, presented a busy scene as bales of newly unloaded merchandise were hoisted up into the loft

17

above. It was obviously a weekday in 1795.

Scarcely aware of what he did, Chris gave a shout of joy, leaning forward, laughter and tears of relief mingled on his face. At least he still held the power to see back through the magic panes into the past time where his good friends lived and moved! There, to his left, were the masts and spars of sailing ships, and Wisconsin Avenue, now Wisconsin no longer but High Street, bustled with men and women in eighteenth-century dress. Chris looked quickly for the masts of the *Mirabelle*, but did not see them at her usual anchorage. He experienced a sharp disappointment that Captain Blizzard and dour Mr. Finney were probably at sea.

He was so taken up with looking out of the bow window at the sunny scene before him that he did not hear the creak of a distant opening door. But when he saw a thin band of sunlight flattening itself on the broad boards beside him, he wheeled at once.

There he stood, the spidery, delicate old man who was William Wicker. His face, minutely wrinkled, was creased in a crackly smile that narrowed the eyes already contracted by the speed of years. The downy white fuzz of what remained of his hair tufted either side of his bald head, and he seemed unstable on his bony legs. But Chris, in his soaring joy at finding his master and old friend, saw only the welcome deep in the dark eyes, and could not see an ancient man, but the strong vigorous one he knew Mr. Wicker to be. Rushing forward to meet him, Chris was momentarily taken aback to find that he was as tall now as the old man himself.

The next moment his young fingers grasped the thin shoulder, only to feel its strength growing under his hand; a broaden-

ing, toughening feel. In the instant of shock before he could draw back to look the magician in the face, Mr. Wicker stood tall and muscular before him, laughing heartily at the boy's inevitable amazement. Mr. Wicker faced Chris in all the vitality and limber strength of his eighteenth-century form, and Chris laughed and choked and clasped his master's hand in thankfulness and confusion.

"Oh, sir! I really thought I might not find you this time — because I so especially wanted to!" He stood off to look at

19

Mr. Wicker, now handsome and spruce. "Gee! It's really good to see you, sir! How've you been?"

The magician put out a lean forceful hand to clap the boy on the shoulder in his turn.

"My good Christopher," he said, "it is indeed splendid to see you! Welcome back! I thank you — I am well — we all are, as you shall see. Come along. I must not tarry here in the shop in my — shall we say — fresher appearance, or a twenti-eth-century shopper would never credit his senses. Bless my soul!" he exclaimed, turning around as he led the way to his sitting room behind the shop. "You have put in all your time at growing, my boy!"

He shut the study door, and Chris, grinning from ear to ear in the fullness of his pleasure at his return, looked happily at the familiar surroundings.

The first time he had seen this cheerful room there had been a fire burning on the hearth, even as it was at that moment. Now, with a nip in the autumn air, the crimson brocade curtains seemed still more lively and warm against approaching winter drafts. The high-backed red leather chairs flung the wink of firelight and sunlight from the brass-headed nails that studded them round; the grandfather clock in the corner clucked and tut-tutted to itself like a dozing old man; the desk with its quill pens still stood between the two windows that looked on Mr. Wicker's garden. Beyond the well-polished panes in front of him Chris could see the turning color of the espaliered trees set against the high brick wall, and admire the gay flower bed that blazed with the red and yellow chrysanthemums that also filled the china bowl on the center table. The intricate design of the fine Indian rug under his feet still pleased the boy with its interlocking colors of blue, red and gold, and to his left at the far end of the room, reaching to the ceiling, stood the carved-wood cupboard where Mr. Wicker kept his books of magic. Chris looked out of the back window for the church on the hill that, in his own time, he knew he would have been able to see. Then, with a smile, he remembered that a hundred years or more must pass before the church would even be built.

He turned back to find his master in his usual place before

21

the fire, his black breeches and coat and closely buttoned waist-coat showing up the freshness of his white muslin stock and neckband; the silver buckles on his shoes as polished as mirrors.

Chris shook his head with a smile. "It's always hard to believe that I'm back, sir," he began. "I enjoy being here so much. It goes as fast — faster — than the vacations between school terms."

Mr. Wicker smiled in return. "Never mind, Christopher. You are here now. Enjoy it. We shall try to spin it out for you this time, if you like."

"What about my clothes, sir?" Chris asked. "May I change into the ones of your century?"

Mr. Wicker gave a gesture with his fine sensitive hand. "There they are, Christopher, awaiting you. I hope that this time they will fit you! You have grown even more than I was prepared for."

Chris laughed. "You can't fool me again, sir! I know they'll fit, no matter how much I've grown!"

He went over to the stool by the big fireplace where a pile of folded clothes lay ready for him. Under the stool a pair of shoes like Mr. Wicker's own stood side by side near the fire. Chris held up the coat and knee breeches.

"Why — they're a new color, sir!" he cried. "I like this brown better than the bluish gray. This color looks like cherry wood."

Mr. Wicker's eyes held his smile.

"The color is more in keeping with your size and age, Christopher," he said. "In 1795 a boy of fourteen is a young man, and expected to behave as such —" He cleared his throat. "As much as possible, of course," he added firmly, turning away at

22

the sight of his pupil's sudden dismay. "Do not worry, Christopher, it will not be too much of a strain on you, I hope!"

As he changed to the clothes of the century in which he now found himself, Chris peppered Mr. Wicker with questions.

"How is Becky, sir? Still as good a cook? And Amos? Has he grown? Taller than I am? What do you know! And Ned? Oh, I'm glad he didn't sail on the *Mirabelle* — I've been missing him. What's that — he got left behind because his adieus to Becky took so long? Well, it takes him quite a while to even reach her cheek, he's so short and she's so big. So he's turned gardener instead? That makes it cozy for Becky, doesn't it? And cozy for Ned, too, of course, so near to the kitchen!"

By the time he had paused to draw breath, Chris was dressed in the knee breeches, linen shirt, waistcoat with brass buttons, and frocked coat of the year 1795. He looked down at his new clothes with satisfaction and wriggled his toes in the handmade shoes.

"All as perfect a fit as usual, sir!" he said with a grin. "They don't even feel strange any more. I think I like them better than ours — more dash, sort of. Well — " he picked up his black three-cornered hat, "can we see the others now, sir, please?"

For answer, Mr. Wicker flung open the door. Down the corridor a deep feminine voice was booming out a sea chantey.

*"What will we do with the drunken sailor —
So early in the morning!"*

Mistress Boozer was in fine voice that day.

23

CHAPTER 4

THE HUGE WOMAN was stirring her steaming kettles and pulling on the chain of the spit where wild duck sent out an appetizing smell, for all the world as if it were only an hour or two since Chris had last left the kitchen. An unguessed number of yards made up her dress of blue and white striped cotton, and enough muslin to curtain a window surrounded her neck and disappeared into her capacious bodice. Her kind cheery face, cheeks aglow with the heat of the fire and perhaps the flutterings of her heart at Ned Cilley's proximity, looked like a full-blown flower. Above it waved and beckoned her legendary hat, its twenty-four roses and twelve waving black plumes nodding and dipping as if superintending from aloft every pinch of salt and tossed-in flavoring.

Beyond her along the wall stood an open kitchen dresser, where shining rows of plates, cups, and saucers made their own flashing display. Behind her, where she stood inside the enormous fireplace — that three standing men could front abreast — was the door giving onto Water Street. On either side of it, Chris saw with relieved feelings, were the two windows as before: the gate-legged table was still opened out in front of the window to the right, and set for a meal. As he stood at the end of the shadowy passage, a third window near him gave light on that side of the room from High Street, together with a glimpse of evergreen shrubs and autumn flowers.

"Oh, what shall we do with the drunken sailor —
So early in the morning!"

bawled Becky, nodding her head and her hat in time to her singing and stirring and tasting without ever losing the beat. Chris began to giggle, remembering the occasion when that particular tune had been forced upon Mistress Boozer's attention as she had been hauled aboard the *Mirabelle* to its rhythm. Memories and affection overcame him, and the boy rushed into the room calling out, "Why — put the man in irons, and walk the lady up!"

"Lord save us and bless us!" shrieked Mistress Boozer, clutching the large spoon she held to her bosom, and then, seeing who it was, burst into happy tears. Throwing her tremendous arms around Chris, she fairly squeezed him flat in the excess of her welcome. On its perch near the table, a gaudy parrot hopped and pranced, recognizing in Chris an old friend.

"By me cap and buttons!" it squawked, mimicking Ned Cilley's voice in a miraculous way. "All I need is a kiss from my Boozer, and a draught or two of ale to keep up me health an' spirits! Spirits! Spirits! Who said spirits?"

Becky's apron corner was quite soaked with her tears, and many were the fond looks she must need give Chris, and turn him all about to admire his tallness and fine air.

She was barely calmed, however, when Chris asked, "Is Amos to be here for dinner, Becky?"

"Mercy on me, yes, unless some untoward accident — saints preserve us! — has come upon him since morning." Becky replied. "He should surely be here at any moment."

"Then," Chris suggested, "let's play a trick on him! When we hear him, I'll get behind you. You straighten his coat collar, and I'll reach around and pull down his jacket or twitch his waistcoat. He won't know where all the hands are coming from!" And suiting the action to the word, Chris took off his jacket and rolled up his sleeves, to make his arms seem like Becky's, who stood watching with her hands on her barrel hips.

"Hump!" she snorted. "Amos is smart. He'll guess some play's afoot, for certain sure!"

"Yes, so he may," Chris retorted, "but not at first, nor from whom."

"No," Becky said, her eyes solemn, "for he hardly dares to expect you, Chris. Hark! I hear him running, now! He does ever be in a hurry for his meals!"

"Small wonder!" Chris whispered, and stepped behind the broad protection of Becky Boozer, who turned her back to the fire, and as Amos threw open the back door appeared to be smoothing down her fichu with elaborate unconcern.

"Hope I'm not late, Miss Becky!" panted Amos, glancing to see if his shoes were clean, under Becky's piercing look. "Heard the clock strike, and think it must be 'bout a hour slow today — my stomach's been at noon for a long while now!"

Becky gave Amos's beaming face a disapproving stare. "Come here, boy, let me straighten down your collar, afore you washes your hands. Closer — there."

Amos, his happy face above his white stock and dark green coat beginning to be puzzled at Becky's sudden solicitude, stood close, looking bewildered at Becky's expressionless face. As she began to pull at the collar of the Negro boy's jacket, which was in perfect order, two other hands gave a jerk to the boy's coat on one side, and to his waistcoat on the other. Total bewilderment flowed over Amos's face as if cold water had been thrown on it. He blinked, his eyes grew large, and feeling extra hands he knew could not be Becky's pulling at his sleeve, and then at his handkerchief, he backed hastily away, stuttering.

"Lor', Miss Becky, there must be ghostses in this place! Else you have extry hands I don't know nothing of! How come you pull my sleeve and yank my coat when I see both your hands on my collar?"

"Tut, Amos," Becky said, tossing her head and her hat.

"Sure, boy, you're mighty fanciful today. I'll turn about slowly, and you shall see there's no one here but you and me."

Becky, ponderous and wide, could have concealed a man behind her, much less a slender boy, and Chris moved slowly as she turned, so that Amos's eyes were larger than ever when he again faced Becky.

" 'Deed they's ghostses — " he began, when all at once he caught sight of the brown jacket Chris had taken off and thrown down on the bench near the fire.

"Who-all's is that?" Amos demanded, pointing. "That's a stranger's coat!"

"Oh no it's not, Amos. It's mine!" Chris shouted, jumping out from behind a guffawing Becky to pound the back of his friend and shake his hand until the fingers of both were sore.

There was much laughter and joy, and Mistress Boozer bustled back to her simmering pots and browning ducks.

"Let's do the same to Ned, when he turns up!" Chris suggested. "Six hands will make him think that other kinds of spirits are possessing him!"

A few minutes later, a great stamping being heard at the door, Amos and Chris hid once more behind Becky, who, flustered at the approach of her admirer, twittered and blushed redder than ever, touching at her bonnet which remained, as usual, immovable.

After a thundering knock on the door which rattled the lock and hinges, Ned peeped coyly around to see if he was expected. At the sight of Mistress Boozer with downcast eyes standing in the middle of the floor, Master Cilley lost no time in whisking inside and closing the door. Fancying himself alone with his belle, Ned, all his snaggle teeth in view, rubbed his knotty hands with glee.

"Why — by me cap an' buttons!" he declared. "Fair lady, you're all expectant-like!"

Poor Amos and Chris, doubled up behind Becky, doubled up still more, holding back their laughter.

"Where's me stool?" demanded Ned. Looking wildly about, he seized it, and pranced over to where Becky modestly awaited him. As he clambered upon the stool in an effort to be on a better level with his heart's desire, Becky, in a fit of emotion — or perhaps merely laughter — covered her face with both her hands. At the same moment Ned felt a pair of arms about his neck, while at the same time, one ear was pinched and his nose was tweaked.

To say that consternation sat upon Master Cilley's honest face would be an understatement of the grossest kind. He stuck his head forward, staring at his loved one's hands, felt of

29

his nose on one side, and of his ear on the other, thereupon the arms about his neck unloosed themselves and gave him a whack on his posterior that caused him to start violently and teeter precariously on the stool. One stocking was then pulled farther down on the slide it had already undertaken by itself; his ruffled hair was scratched with vigor, until still staring at Mistress Boozer's hands, Ned Cilley gave a howl of horror and fright, and bolting off the stool, rushed pell-mell out the door.

Long and loud were the shouts of laughter from Amos and Chris, until poor Ned, hearing the commotion inside, ventured to flatten his nose against the window to see what went on. The sight of a missed and well-loved boy brought him pelting back in again to join in the general hilarity as gustily as though it were not at his own expense.

Becky, however, her warm heart torn between amusement and not wanting to hurt the "delikit feelin's" of her gallant, lightly boxed the ears of the two boys to calm them down, and sent them to the washtub corner to clean up before the meal.

"Eh!" cried Ned, falling exhausted into his usual chair at the table, "that was something I should never have fathomed out — not I! Them hands a-pulling and a-pushing and a-prying! Even to giving me old noggin a good scratch!" At the thought, Ned scratched his head once more until his hair stood up like the quills on a porcupine. "Mistress Becky, fie and for shame — a-terrifyin' your own dear! Come, now, I never did get a kiss from my Boozer!" And the persistent Ned jumped up to run over to where Becky laughed and stirred and laughed again. But cooking was a fine art with Becky, and all was coming to the exact point where every dish was cooked to a turn. So she pushed Ned off with scant ceremony.

"Get along with you!" she said. "Fie, yourself! Do you
distract me now, Ned Cilley, sure and your fine dinner will
be burnt to a crisp, and what a heart's pity *that* would be! Tush!
Sit down now, every one of you. Such goings-on. Gets a body
all churned about — and you with such a delikit stummick,
Master Cilley. How shall you be able to eat a bite or a morsel,
answer me that?"

At her first words Ned had scurried back to his chair, and
now, grasping his knife and fork in his two fists, waited with
every evidence of a monstrous appetite, while wagging his

head in a deprecating way.

"You never spoke truer word, my lovely lass," he replied in a sober tone. "Indeed, my stummick was peevish, earlier today, and now, with all this excitement and flustering and blustering, I doubt well that no more than a crumb shall I be able to swallow."

"There now," commiserated Becky, as she began to bring dish after dish to the table, "what did I say? All the fault of this dear boy. You must try to eat, Master Cilley, to show there's no hard feelings. There — try a bite, do."

Before Amos, Ned and Chris, the surface of the large table vanished under the weight of a roast of beef, a lamb stew with potatoes and turnips, a duck apiece, wild rice, fresh bread, puddings, pies, open tarts, cheeses, pickles, and sauces. Mistress Boozer stood by uneasily, looking from face to face, to see if she had failed, somehow, to tempt a lagging appetite.

"A bite," she urged, "a taste, or I shall never live it down. Ned — a spoonful — "

But this time it was not Ned who raised his bushy eyebrows in his signal of old. It was Chris, his appetite outrunning for once Ned Cilley's, who called out, "Every man for himself!" and reached forward.

CHAPTER 5

*B*ACK IN MR. Wicker's sitting room Chris wagged his head in imitation of Ned.

"Well, I *did* just manage a bite and a morsel, sir!" he said. "Why you don't get fat on Becky's wonderful food, I shall never know."

Mr. Wicker, comfortable in his red leather chair, his long legs stretched out toward the somnolent blaze, looked up at the boy standing tall before him.

"Was all as good as ever, Christopher?" he inquired. Chris shook his head gravely.

"No sir. It was better!" he asserted. Then, the remembrance of his drive of the day before came back to him and he sat down abruptly in the red chair opposite, pulling it a trifle closer to Mr. Wicker in a confidential way.

"Sir," he began, "there is something on my mind that happened yesterday, and that I wanted to ask you about. It was one of the main reasons for my coming." He hesitated, casting about in his mind for the point at which he wanted to begin.

"We were driving down near the Shenandoah —" he commenced, when all at once there was a sudden sharp peal at the bell. It jangled, bobbing on its spring, just above Mr. Wicker's study door, and both master and pupil turned, startled, to look at it. The inanimate thing seemed to speak and wave at them to obtain their immediate attention.

"Dear me!" Mr. Wicker said with a sigh. "I was not expecting callers. Run and see who it is, Christopher, there's a good lad."

Chris went out toward the door of the shop. Behind him as he went he heard a second, more determined ring. It reminded him of a gusty night, a year or so before, when a Georgetown neighbor, Colonel Moffit, had appeared at Mr. Wicker's door. The result of that nocturnal visit had been an unexpected and almost too exciting adventure. As Chris hurried forward he felt the same beating in the air, something of urgency, unease, and fear, that he remembered having been touched by on that earlier occasion.

Opening the door he found himself confronted by a pink-cheeked old lady in a voluminous taffeta gown, a long black cape trailing to the ground from her shoulders; a frilled white muslin cap confining her gray hair. Her hands, in black lace mittens, were folded tightly over her waist, and her mouth was set in a straight narrow line. A pair of bright eyes looked Chris up and down, and then recognition lit them. Her face relaxed into a cheerful and engaging smile, and she gave a brisk nod.

"Why, it is Christopher Mason, if I am not mistook. Good afternoon to you, my boy. You must have made a long voyage — we have not seen you hereabouts for many a month."

Chris smiled back. He remembered old Mrs. Moffit well,

34

grandmother of a pretty girl called Susan and the mother of the same Colonel Moffit to whom he had opened the door that distant windy night.

"Good afternoon, ma'am. Yes, I did go rather far," he replied with a smile, "but here I am back again."

"Is Mr. Wicker at home?" demanded Mrs. Moffit, standing as straight and as high as her short height would allow. Behind her a heavy country coach waited, while four well-groomed horses champed with clinking noises at their bits. Looking up,

Chris saw a smiling old Negro on the box whom he also remembered: Uncle Borb. Chris nodded a greeting, and looked quickly back to Mrs. Moffit.

"Yes ma'am, he is. Will you come in?"

Mrs. Moffit lost no time, darting forward as energetically as a woman of half her age.

"Yes, indeed I will!" she declared, sweeping past Chris with a rustle of silk and a fresh smell of rose-geranium. Chris waved at Uncle Borb, who was clambering down to stand at the horses' heads. As Chris turned to follow Mrs. Moffit he found that she had already reached the study door and had been greeted by Mr. Wicker. The lean quiet man was about to shut the door behind her when she stayed him with a gesture.

"One moment, Mr. Wicker, sir. What I have to say, I should like taken down, and a witness to it." She glanced keenly at Chris. "I do not know about this lad." Her face was thoughtful. "Not that he may be too young, but — " Her eyes moved quickly to Mr. Wicker's face.

"I understand you I believe, Mrs. Moffit," her host said, answering her look. "Christopher here is thoroughly trustworthy, even though his years be few." His face eased from soberness into a smile. "I have proof of his loyalty over many years. Whatever you have to say will be safe with him, I venture to say, as with myself."

Mrs. Moffit gave him a long piercing study. Then her mouth relaxed from its taut thin line, and a faint relief showed in her face.

"I need no better assurance than *that*, sir," she said. "And he writes well — a good hand?"

Mr. Wicker's look sprang to Chris's and a twinkle sparked in

36

the eyes of both. Chris knew that his master had no great opinion of the twentieth-century style of writing.

"Tolerable, ma'am, tolerable."

Mrs. Moffit gave a movement of her shoulders indicative of her growing satisfaction.

"Then he may take down a document that I wish left in your safekeeping?" she asked tranquilly, looking toward the door of the study.

"Most certainly, Mrs. Moffit," Mr. Wicker assured her. "Come in then, Christopher, and be seated at the desk. You will find paper, quill, ink, and sandshaker there. Mrs. Moffit will tell you what she wants recorded, and when."

Chris knew that quite some ceremony remained to be carried out before they should hear what Mrs. Moffit had to say, and he waited impatiently while Mr. Wicker pulled at a bell rope hanging near his desk, after settling Mrs. Moffit in the place of honor near the fire. Chris, watching her, thought what a fine portrait she would have made just as she was then: white cap with gray ribbons, gray silk dress and black cape, and her fine, alert, distinguished face that held so much of determination and wisdom. The soft red of the leather chair framed her with a complimentary and harmonious background.

Becky Boozer came into the room in answer to the bell, and in a moment, a rare aged Madeira wine, accompanied by a plate of Becky's lightest cakes, stood on a small table at Mrs. Moffit's elbow. The guest looked at her amber-filled glass absently and did not touch it at once. Instead, she waited with her mittened hands folded in her lap and her eyes on the fire for Becky to withdraw. When the door was finally closed upon this elephantine person, Mrs. Moffit sighed. Leaning against the back

37

of her chair, she seemed more at ease. She unfolded her hands and made a light gesture.

"Mr. Wicker," she began, "we have known one another for many years." She shook her head, as if humorously reproving the passage of time, and looked up again quickly, her eyes very clear. "What exactly do you think of me?"

Mr. Wicker seemed only mildly taken aback. He smiled, his fingertips together, looking at his guest over the top of them with amusement in his eyes.

"Now, now, Mrs. Moffit!" he chided. "Fishing for compliments so early in the day?"

Mrs. Moffit tossed her head with impatience and did not smile. "I am serious, Mr. Wicker. Humor me, I beg of you. What sort of a woman do I give the impression of being, pray answer me that?"

Mr. Wicker's jocosity vanished. Chris, sitting almost forgotten in the shadow between the windows, saw his master sit up straighter, his face serious.

"Very well, ma'am, since you ask it," he said in his deep voice. "We have indeed known one another for many years. During that time I have seen your firmness and resolve grow after the death of your husband, and have not only heard of the remarkable manner in which you manage your plantation Riveridge — "

Chris gave a start.

" — but I have seen there, for myself, your ability in making your plantation perhaps the best in that part of the country. Certainly," he went on, looking across at his guest, "you know as well as I that scarcely a month goes by without a visitor coming from far to see the success of your methods and the im-

provements you have made over old systems. They observe, learn, and in their turn, improve their own properties." He leaned back, his fingertips together again. Reflectively, he went on. "I should say of you, Martha Moffit," he said slowly, as if measuring his words, "that you are a woman of determination and vision, not lacking in humor; with firmness, justice, and tolerance toward those working for you. In short, an intelligent realist."

"Aha!" Mrs. Moffit looked relieved. "A realist." She nodded her head as if she had been in some doubt on this point. "You do my character much kindness, William Wicker, and throughout you make no mention of fancy." She faced him with piercing attention. "Would you call me in any way a fanciful woman, Mr. Wicker?"

As she spoke she sat forward. A great deal seemed to depend on the reply her host should give her. Mr. Wicker shook his head slowly, not taking his eyes from the unrelenting scrutiny of his visitor.

"No, Mrs. Moffit, ma'am. That I should never call you. You have never, in the years through which I have known you, been in any way a fanciful woman."

Mrs. Moffit fell back in her chair, her face even more troubled than before, and shifted her glance away to the fire.

"Then what I have to tell you is perhaps even worse than I had anticipated," she said. "For while I did not imagine that I could be fanciful, yet in a way — " a small capable hand in its black lace mitten gave a helpless feminine motion, " — in a way I hoped I might be becoming so, in my old age."

She sighed heavily, shaking her head. Mr. Wicker leaned toward her, evidently concerned.

"Come now, ma'am. Take a sip of your wine and unburden yourself of what troubles you." He nodded in Chris's direction, to where the boy sat on the edge of his chair by the desk. "The boy there is not like most, but will guard whatever you choose to say with silence and discretion. You may depend upon it."

Without warning, to the acute embarrassment of both the man and the boy, Mrs. Moffit burst into quiet tears, pulled a minute lace-edged handkerchief from her silk reticule, and dabbed at her eyes.

"Forgive me," she said in a small voice. "I find myself suddenly so relieved at being able to share what has become an absorbing anxiety." She blew her nose with a return of her usual energy, and put her handkerchief firmly away. "There have been times, Mr. Wicker," she said, "when I have doubted my own sanity. I need your help and advice as never before, and know that somehow you will be able to help me."

She put one hand on the arm of her chair, and threw back her cape as if what she had to tell would be long in the telling.

"It concerns a neighbor of mine, near the plantation," she began, "near Riveridge. A newcomer, by name Claggett Chew," confided Mrs. Moffit.

41

CHAPTER 6

HE SITTING ROOM where the three people sat, usually so cheerful, seemed so no longer. The afternoon was aging and the autumn light, bright before, was withering quickly from the sky, leaving a chill flat sheen that shone coldly over the garden, blanching to dullness the warm crimson of the curtains. As Mrs. Moffit had spoken the name dreaded, feared, and well known, Chris had caught his breath with an audible gasp. A silence lasted for a full minute, in which even the sound of the big clock seemed stilled. Mrs. Moffit swung in her chair to face Chris in the gathering dusk.

"You know this man?" she asked. "It would appear so. His name would seem known to you."

Chris swallowed, his knees weak, even though he was sitting down. "Yes ma'am," he gulped out, "I've had some meetings with him."

Mrs. Moffit paused a moment before speaking once more. Not much escaped the shrewd old woman. She looked long at Chris's face before she turned away.

"Humph!" she exploded. "I gather you found him no pleasanter than anyone else has. A singularly disagreeable individual, that Chew." She pinned Mr. Wicker with one of her sharpest looks. "Some men say, Mr. Wicker, that Claggett Chew has been a pirate in his time."

But although she searched her host's face, Mr. Wicker remained impassive.

"Rumor says many things, ma'am," he remarked drily, and Mrs. Moffit could see that this was all she would get from him on that subject.

"Very well," she said with some asperity, "so you choose to make no remark. That is your business, sir. I do not doubt but that you know more of Claggett Chew than any of the rest of us, but I respect your silence — you probably have a reason for it."

She patted her billowing silk skirts, took a placid sip of her wine, with a slowness calculated to irritate her listeners and give her their full attention before she went on.

"This person Chew," Mrs. Moffit said, "has taken over the small house some say he, or one Gosler, built many years ago, and then half abandoned. It stands at a bend of Dragon Run, a goodly stream that passes by below Colonel Charles Washington's house, Happy Retreat, and coming through the woods and pastures, is fed by other springs, until it falls into the Shenandoah a mile below Riveridge."

She hesitated, looking into the fire.

"This Claggett Chew has begun a dyeing works in a new wing built on to his house. He has added a large chimney, and built a considerable shed for the drying of the dyed stuffs and the packaging of them below. So far as I know, he may have a

43

good trade." She looked at Mr. Wicker who was all attention, his quiet gaze never leaving her face. "This is not what has concerned me," Mrs. Moffit stated. Chris and Mr. Wicker waited for their guest to take her own time. Well governed as Mrs. Moffit's feelings usually were, both the magician and his pupil could see that the good lady was laboring under a considerable strain. Presently she continued.

"I have a large plantation as you know, Mr. Wicker," she said. "We produce at Riveridge everything we need, from food to cotton and wool-stuffs, and it has been my practice to dye my own materials. We have our own gristmill, and are self-supporting, with the exception of a few luxuries."

As she stared into the flames Chris could see beyond the indomitable will of the old woman a great sweetness too, and for a passing second he guessed how pretty and winning she must have been as a girl.

"To run my many projects," Mrs. Moffit went on, "I have many workers, Mr. Wicker, but no slaves." Her head came up with a proud lift. "My husband never did approve of this abominable practice, and no more do I. Some of my people call themselves slaves, and it is true that if I need additional workers I am obliged to buy them. But there all semblance to slavery stops. They work for me, and stay or go, of their own free will. I am happy to say they seem to be so well content that the majority are descendants of the families who first came to us. They feel that they "belong," not by slavery but by affection, to me and to Riveridge. They take a great pride in the success of every plan, and I attempt to train every man and woman to the type of work for which they seem best fitted. In return for their time and labor, I care for them as if they were my own

44

kin. Doctor and nurse them when they fall sick; clothe them
— and clothe them well; and feed them the same food that I
eat myself. Why not? They are unfortunate creatures
wrenched from their own soil. I feel ashamed, deeply ashamed,
that we should so dare to treat a weaker race." Her fine
eyes sparked with temper, and her cheeks grew rosier. "Well,"
she went on more calmly, "they know they have a haven with
me, and I can seldom find fault with what they give me in return. There!" she said, almost defiantly. "Now you know
my views on slavery! But of course all who speak with me dis-

cover my mind only too easily — I can never contain myself on the subject!"

Mr. Wicker permitted himself a smile. "You are an admirable woman, Martha Moffit," he told her. "Born just a little ahead of your time."

Mrs. Moffit flashed him a look. "Humph! Then you think as I do — that men of good heart will not permit slavery to continue long?"

Mr. Wicker shook his head. "Not long, perhaps," he ventured, "but that short will still be too long." His eyes seemed on a distant vision that only he could see. "Sorrow and misery will breed only their own likenesses. Much of these will grow in this land before others come to feel as you do, ma'am."

"Well," said Mrs. Moffit, drawing herself up and flicking her head with a positive gesture, "all I know is, I shall have no part of it. That is what I have to say, in a manner of speaking, to you now, William Wicker."

Chris decided that Mrs. Moffit was not only a good landowner but a woman of considerable force, and that once she had set her mind to righting a wrong she was not likely to be dissuaded from it. She would win the goal she had set herself, no matter how difficult.

"Mr. Wicker," she was saying, "that man Chew not only has slaves for his fields — he grows large crops — but they behave in a most singular way."

The room was nearly dark, except for the washed gray beyond the windows and the surly glow of the fire. Almost nothing could be seen now of Mr. Wicker or Mrs. Moffit except their silhouettes against the red gleam from the hearth, and so absorbed were the three people that no one had thought of

lighting a candle. Mrs. Moffit's voice, low and fast, took up her story again.

"I have seen those men working in the fields, and I know Negroes — these do not behave as any Negroes that I ever saw before, and I have known many." She leaned forward to tap Mr. Wicker's knee with a slender finger for emphasis. "Those men stumble along the furrows or behind a plow, or with a spade, as if they were ill — or asleep. Or dying!" She caught her breath at the remembrance. "I have spoken to them when they happened near the road. Their eyes seem blind; they seemed not to hear me, for they did not answer. And Claggett Chew, seeing me speak to one of those men once, strode out of his house shouting, and cracking that horrible whip he carries, so that it frightened my horses, who are unused to a goad. They fairly bolted away before I could get any reply, either from Chew or from his slave."

In the darkness her voice penetrated to the farthest corner, striking Chris with a cold ache of terror and wonderment.

"Nor is that all. Strange things go on at night within the ell

47

of that building of Chew's," she said. "Fires are built in what is almost an enclosed courtyard, what with the stream flowing on the two other sides, for it makes a turn just by the long building. Shrieks and cries and sorrowful songs sound out in the night, so my own people say, though I can get them to tell me little of what transpires. They seem increasingly frightened and are beginning to tell me nothing."

She stopped as if gathering strength for what she had to say at the last.

"Recently, Mr. Wicker, I have waked in the night to see a dreadful — a terrible — thing at my window. And my window is on the second floor. I have seen a monster's face — a monster with horns!" She flung out her hands in supplication. "Oh — do not disbelieve me," she cried, "as I disbelieved even my own eyes! For yesterday, the night being cool, I could see that it lived. Its breath steamed upon my windowpane!"

CHAPTER 7

*M*R. *WICKER, WITH A* quick movement, thrust a thin wax taper into the fire, and an instant later candles sent out their reassuring light from all sides of the room. Pouring out a fresh glass of wine for Mrs. Moffit, Mr. Wicker urged her to drink it, and at his gesture, Chris drew the heavy brocade curtains close. The room, in a twinkling, assumed a cozy air. A part of the dark terrors that Mrs. Moffit had seen and felt, and had communicated to her two listeners, receded, though not far. The poor lady's face was pale, and she chafed her hands and drew her cloak about her as if a chill enveloped her. Chris threw more wood on the fire; the lowering brands flared up and a measure of comfort was restored.

Mrs. Moffit looked entreatingly up at her host when she had somewhat recovered herself.

"It sounds like madness, does it not, Mr. Wicker?" she asked. "The face of a monster at Riveridge, and at my very window! Twenty feet or more above the ground! Perhaps you do not believe anything so wild, so lacking in reason?" Her look and her voice begged for some reassurance.

"Calm yourself, Mrs. Moffit," Mr. Wicker soothed her. "I do believe you, and do have some idea of what this all may be. Nevertheless," he said in a serious tone, "it may well mean also that some harm is intended, if not to you, then directed at the others on the plantation. You should have protection. These occurrences should be observed to see what lies behind them."

Mrs. Moffit instantly took heart. Her color began to return.

"Exactly!" she exclaimed. "But you see, my son is away for several months, and I do not wish to alarm David and Susie. You remember my granddaughter only too well, I am afraid, Mr. Wicker," Mrs. Moffit said with a faint smile. "She was the cause of much trouble to you, I am well aware." She sighed. "They live — she and her husband, David Russell — on a continuation of the plantation in a house they have only just completed. Their son is but a few months old. I do not like to trouble young people who are happy and busy about their lives, with the fears and alarms of the old."

She looked earnestly at Mr. Wicker, standing before her with his back to the fire and his face intent. "I do not like to impose on a friendship, Mr. Wicker, but I should take it with the greatest and most profound gratitude if you could spare me a little of your time and presence, and come to Riveridge until my son returns." She spread out her hands, and they looked very small on the sea of gray taffeta. "We have a sizable guest wing at Riveridge, where I shall see that you are made comfortable." The old lady searched her friend's face above her. "You could say that you had papers to write, and were seeking the tranquillity of the country — God save us! — to do so." She glanced at Chris. "Bring the boy along," she added. "He seems sensible and lively. It may be that he shall discover more than any of us — a great deal is in the hands of the young. What do you say, William Wicker? Can you oblige me? I should take it as real charity on your part if you can spare the time. I know you to be a busy man. I do not ask this of you lightly."

Mr. Wicker looked down at Martha Moffit gently, and all the deep kindness of his heart and the wisdom of his mind were there to be seen for those who could find them.

"Of course I shall oblige you, ma'am," he said. "I could not allow you to return alone under these incredible conditions. I shall be most happy to stay with you, and shall make my arrangements this very night." He looked over to Chris, saying in an offhand tone, "Do you think you would care to accompany me, my boy?"

The expression on Chris's face was ample answer.

An hour later Mrs. Moffit was ready to take her departure. A document had been carefully taken down by Chris — with some effort, due to his never having used a quill pen before.

51

The paper was duly witnessed by Mr. Wicker, Ned, and Becky, and locked away in a strongbox. When all this had been done Mrs. Moffit's face showed her relief. She smiled for the first time that afternoon with genuine warmth.

"There now!" she cried, "I feel a deal better, knowing that should anything untoward happen to me the facts are there, as I have seen them, and whatever villainous thing or person may be afoot, justice can be done. For never, in all my years at Riveridge — " and Mrs. Moffit raised her mittened hands and rolled up her eyes in scandalized horror, " — never have such goings-on disturbed our countryside before."

She nodded her bonnet emphatically at Mr. Wicker as she rose to go.

"I have small doubt myself, William Wicker, that that man Chew was, or is, or shall be again, a pirate. If ever a man looked the part!" Up went her hands and eyes once more. "La! of all the places the rogue could choose to go, he needs must choose my neighborhood! Well," and she turned in the doorway to make her adieus, her silk dress and silk-lined cape whispering after her like two gossips as she moved away across the the floor, "I feel much improved for my afternoon, Mr. Wicker, sir, and I do thank you for it. My stay has proved overlong, I fear, but there was reason enough for that, and I have every hope of forgiveness!" She gave Mr. Wicker a dazzling smile, and all at once Chris saw where her beguiling granddaughter Susie got her charming ways.

Mr. Wicker helped his spry guest into her coach. She promptly put her head out the window.

"That's understood, then. I shall send Uncle Borb's son, young Jonah, on ahead tonight to the house with the orders, and you may start whenever it is convenient to you. You are bound to pass me — this coach will take two days to get there, stopping overnight at Leesburg, and perhaps the second night at the house of relations. The roads are not good. Yet I fancy that we shall arrive at more or less the same time. Your boxes and luggage can be sent over to our house here at Cherry Lane early tomorrow, by Amos, and he shall take Jonah's place and ride beside Uncle Borb." She shook her capped head. " 'Tis not wise to have only one man on the box for so long a journey. Two is wiser." She waved a hand. "Thank you from my heart, my dear friend. I knew I could count on you!" Then, raising her voice to carry up to the box where Uncle Borb sat patiently, the reins in his hands, she called out, "Very well, Uncle Borb, you may take me home, now!" And off rolled the coach to the nearby Moffit town house with a grinding of wheels and a good smell of harness and horseflesh.

The night was turning chill, but Mr. Wicker and Chris stood

in the freshening wind watching the heavy coach roll away.

"A woman of many facets," said Mr. Wicker carefully at last, and in a thoughtful way.

"Sir — " Chris asked, "the name of the stream, Dragon Run —" He pondered a moment while Mr. Wicker looked about, at the night sky, at the somber sleep-wrapped houses of Georgetown, and waited. "It's a strange name, sir," the boy commented. "How did it get that name, do you know?"

Mr. Wicker's attention came back to Chris from distant places.

"There is a legend about it Christopher, so I understand. Mrs. Moffit told me of it once when I was visiting Riveridge. The legend goes that a dragon lived near where the stream is now. That it was in the habit of going down to the Shenandoah to drink, and that its heavy tail, dragging behind it over the same way, in time marked out what is now the stream bed. For it is said that the stream lay, in earlier times, farther to the south. But in time of flood the water ran into the weaving trail that literally was a 'dragon run'." He smiled at Chris's absorbed face. "A run is also a stream, in that part of the country, Christopher. It is only a legend. Someone doubtless made it up to while away the hours of a stormy night at a tavern. A traveler who had heard of such things, who knows?"

Chris did not accept this explanation. "It just *could* be true, couldn't it, sir?"

Mr. Wicker shifted, preparatory to moving indoors.

"Everything is possible, Christopher. Prehistoric animals wandered the world at one time. The legend may be an Indian tale. Well — Mrs. Moffit repeated it to me as I have told it to you." A reminiscent smile hovered over Mr. Wicker's mouth.

54

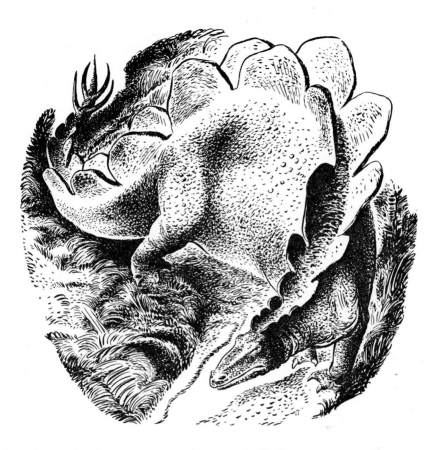

"A remarkable woman, Martha Moffit."

"She has a man-sized job, all right," Chris answered admiringly. "With all she must get done on her plantation!"

"Yes, my boy," Mr. Wicker replied, going back indoors, "but she has a woman's courage and a woman's heart. When those are good, my boy," said Mr. Wicker, holding up the lantern, "there are none finer! Come now, we must have a bite of supper and then pack our necessities, for you and I shall make an early start, at sunup tomorrow. For Leesburg, and for Riveridge!"

CHAPTER 8

HE SUN WAS BARELY up when Chris and Mr. Wicker, astride two good horses, started out from Georgetown. Freshness lay everywhere, for Georgetown then was little more than a country village, with more fields, gardens, and spreading trees than houses. Rooftops were now varnished with sun. Becky, Amos, and Ned waved to the two travelers as they set out up High Street on the sidling, frisky mounts. Amos had Mr. Wicker's barrel-topped trunks piled on a wheelbarrow, ready to take over to Colonel Moffit's house, and from there to ride along to Riveridge beside Uncle Borb, butler and coachman for twenty years to the Moffit family.

The way to Leesburg, so easily reached for Chris by car only two days before, was a new and far lengthier experience in 1795. The road itself was rutted and muddy, where it was not deep in red Virginia dust. Houses were few and far between, and most were placed near the road so that what little life and movement there was could be seen, and visitors encouraged to come in.

The man and the boy rode steadily, and at length were considering opening their leather saddlebags for the meat and bread and flask of watered wine that Becky had prepared for them, when they approached a fine plantation house set at a little distance back from the highroad. Sitting near the gate, chewing a straw and enjoying the autumn sun, sat an old Negro. As the two riders approached he eyed them keenly, and when they drew level with the gate, rose, taking off his hat with a bow.

"Morning, sir and young master! My master, Mr. John Pillar, do present his compliments to you two gentlemen, and begs will you favor him with your company at dinner? Food's about ready to come to the table." He smiled broadly, and as a further encouragement, said, "Sun's growing warm, and road's mighty dusty today. Master'd take your company as a favor —"

Mr. Wicker, having reined his horse and listened to what the old man had to say, smiled in return.

"Why, Mr. Pillar is most kind," he returned. "We shall be very pleased to accept his hospitality. Do you go on ahead to the house; we will dismount here and stretch our legs while leading in our horses. Please to tell Mr. Pillar that William Wicker and Christopher Mason send their compliments and thanks, and bid him a good morning!"

So saying, Mr. Wicker dismounted. The Negro hurried ahead down the avenue of trees to the fine house glimpsed at its end. Chris, his horse's reins in his hand, looked inquiringly at Mr. Wicker.

"What's this, sir? You know this man?"

Mr. Wicker's lips gave the hint of a smile. "No, Christopher, but since you are in another century, I thought you might be interested in its customs — to say nothing of the fact that the

58

invitation falls at just the right time, does it not? No," he continued, leading his fox mare forward up the avenue, "you must remember that there are no radios, television, few newspapers in this time. No easy means of getting about. It is quite customary in this part of the world for a man who would like news from the town to post his most trusted servant at the gate. You would be surprised, perhaps," Mr. Wicker went on, "at what remarkable judges of character and of people Negroes are. They have had to be, I expect, to sense the moods and whims of their masters. They also have an excellent intuition. We are being offered what will undoubtedly be a delicious meal, in return for all the news we can think of. And I fancy that we shall also find that the colored butler is a good judge. I am confident that we shall like our host, as I hope he will like us."

So it proved, and a pleasant hour or so later, two much refreshed people continued their journey. Their host, a scholarly man much tied to the overseeing of his lands, sped them on their way, standing on the steps before his door. Chris's eyes caught the glint of amusement and satisfaction in the face of the old butler, who had withdrawn deferentially a little way past his master.

Chris grinned. "That was certainly a wonderful lunch!" He shook his head as he trotted beside his teacher. "There are all kinds of magic, sir, aren't there?"

"No doubt about it, Christopher my boy!" his smiling companion replied, and on they went, slowed now by herds of cattle being driven to market, flocks of geese, or by the swaying two-wheeled shay, rapid and light, of some journeying landowner and his groom on their way to a neighborhood stock sale. More infrequently they drew rein as a rocking coach thundered by.

Leesburg was reached at dusk. Both travelers were splattered from fording streams, and covered with dust as they came to the inn.

"It won't be hard to sleep tonight!" Chris announced as they drew up their weary horses. "In fact, I may drop on my face any minute now!" As he got carefully down from his horse Mr. Wicker gave him a thoughtful look.

"Sleep if you wish, Christopher. I intend taking a fresh horse and pushing on to reconnoiter." At Chris's dismayed expression Mr. Wicker clapped him heartily on the shoulder. "Do not be so cast down, my poor lad! I shall mix you that liquid to drink that will wipe out not only your fatigue but all need of sleep."

Chris brightened somewhat but not entirely. "That liquid is fine, Mr. Wicker," he said dubiously. "I remember how well it works. It isn't only that I'm sleepy. It's that — well —" He looked embarrassed. "I haven't done any riding in a long time, and outside of feeling that I'm going to be bandy-legged for the rest of my life, I don't think I can sit down on anything for quite a while!"

Mr. Wicker threw back his head and indulged in one of his rare but infectious laughs. The colored ostlers and grooms in the courtyard of the inn were laughing too. They laughed just for the fun of it, not caring whether there was a reason or not, and Chris, stiff and tired though he was, could not resist joining in.

"Dear me!" the magician gasped at last, "I have not had a laugh like that in a long time! Never fear, Christopher, I have a salve that will not only permit you to sit on a horse, but allow you to enjoy the ride! But first, let us wash some of the travel stains away, and eat a little supper. Then we shall see what we shall see, on the other side of the mountain."

The night was far advanced when Mr. Wicker and Chris, allowing the horses to pick their own way in the dark, at length came out of the forest of the Blue Ridge into the faint starlight at the river's edge.

"We must be above the bridge," Chris said, as his horse bent his head to the water. "I don't recognize this place."

Mr. Wicker's voice came back to him from the shadow a few feet away.

"There is no bridge, Christopher. This is Vestal's Landing, and there is a ferry, I believe. But I prefer to keep our arrival strictly to ourselves, if possible, and not disturb the boatman. This is where the bridge is to be one day, right enough. What I propose is to ford the river a little higher up. We may have wet feet, but it cannot be helped." There was a rustling of branches on Chris's left as Mr. Wicker and his mount pushed through, and the magician's voice drifted back to him. "Turn your horse and follow me. There is a game trail here that runs along the bank and, higher up, a reasonable fording place."

The Shenandoah moved glossily on their right, black and silver where the slight gleam of the September stars touched it. The only sound was the water's rush over its stony bed, and now and again the startled cry of some nightbird, disturbed in its sleeping. Only a few hundred yards above where Chris in his own time had driven across the river on the modern bridge, Mr. Wicker drew up and waited for his pupil.

The river made a bend under the mountain, and there the
hillside became too steep and precipitous for riders to go up it.

"Here, I think," Mr. Wicker said. "Follow me."

The horses gingerly took their way down the steep bank,
tried the footing in the river and started across. At no time was
the water so high that the horses had to swim, and by tucking
up his legs, Chris kept his boots dry. In a short time the two
were on the opposite shore.

Mr. Wicker led the way up through fields and over grassy
slopes.

"What I hope to do is to reach a high position from which
we can see something of our friend Mr. Chew's house, without
crossing the road."

"No friend of mine, sir!" Chris refuted hotly. "Nor of yours, either, I'm pretty sure! Do you think you know what he is up to this time?"

"Yes, Christopher," Mr. Wicker's voice came back huskily. A carrying silence hung over the open space they were then crossing. "But I am not sure enough to discuss it. That must wait. Here — this hilltop appears to be unfenced. Do you hear the sound of a stream? We are coming to it — "

"Dragon Run!" Chris muttered to himself, and as he said the words the damp coolness of the running water brushed against his cheek like the moist hand of a child. "This *is* Dragon Run, sir?" he asked, raising his voice to where he could dimly see the neat black figure astride his horse ahead of him.

"Hush lad!" came Mr. Wicker's answer, but such was his ability that the words sounded close at Chris's ear, and the boy knew that no sound had escaped the magician's lips to disturb the quiet. Just within the shadow of the trees and brush that followed the stream, Chris could see that his master was dismounting. He therefore did likewise, leading his horse up to where the magician stood waiting for him.

"We are well below the bridge that crosses Dragon Run," Mr. Wicker said in a scarcely audible tone. "The bridge is just below Chew's house. I propose to ford the stream here, and lead the horses carefully and as silently as possible, up the hill in front of us. From its top we may be able to get a good view."

"At *night*, sir?" Chris ejaculated, incredulous. He received a low chuckle for most of his reply.

"You give me little credit, do you not, Christopher? I still possess a magic trick or two! Come. I am afraid that this time you will have to get your feet wet. Go forward carefully. The stream is not deep. I am hopeful that the sound of the water over the stones will cover any careless knock of hoof, or stumble."

Leading the way, the magician stepped into the swiftly running water. His black clothes and dark hair seemed to melt into the night, and unless Chris had been close at his heels he would never have seen him. The horses entered the stream beside their riders, but halfway across Mr. Wicker's mount lifted its head, sniffed the wind, and pricked up its ears. The magician put his hand softly over the nose of the animal and the whinny it had been about to give was stilled in time.

The shadow under the trees was almost total. Sudden lines

64

of starlight on a long branch or curved tree trunk gave Chris the heart-thumping impression of silent men holding deadly weapons, ready for the moment to overcome both his companion and himself. He seemed to see one flattened against a tree bole there, and another peering from around a limb at his very elbow, so that it was with a long outbreath of relief that he felt the ground rising under his feet as they began to climb the hill. As they went up the trees were left below, where they outlined the water.

The night had cleared and at once, coming from the intense dark, Chris began to worry that it was indeed too clear — that they might too easily be seen. However, Mr. Wicker's tall muscular figure moved on ahead, going from clump to clump of bushes, or moving quickly into the black cast by isolated trees.

It seemed no time before they reached the top of the hill, coming up it from behind. The sound of Dragon Run reached them only faintly now, and as Chris looked about, the hilltop appeared to him to be exposed and treeless.

"Look, Christopher!" whispered Mr. Wicker, touching his arm. "Something does indeed seem to be going on behind those walls!"

Below him, five hundred yards away, lay the L shape of a low house, pale in the night. It was the very house Chris and his parents had seen two days before. Now, from the hidden courtyard made and completed by the natural walls of trees and the stream, a well of light flowed up. As if borne on the reddish glow, a confused sound of shouting, cries, and low drums was carried up to the two watchers on the wind-swept hill.

CHAPTER 9

HAT IN THE world!" Chris murmured, looking this way and that to see better. "Some sort of ceremony, sir?"

"It would seem so," Mr. Wicker replied softly. "Here Christopher, is something you have never used before."

The magician pulled from his pocket a small round object. Pulling on it, he lengthened it in a trice into a spyglass. Chris's eyes opened wider.

"Why — that looks like the spyglass I won from Simon Gosler, the old humpbacked miser! Claggett Chew's crony."

"No, Christopher. This has a difference. Try it and see."

Chris took the glass into his hands but gave a look into his master's ironic face.

"Ultraviolet ray, sir?"

"Not exactly, my boy," Mr. Wicker answered. "The same principle, differently applied."

Chris, watching the mixing of shadows and firelight that trembled and shifted behind the walls of the white-painted house,

66

was only half listening. "I'm sure I should never understand it, in my century or yours, sir," he said, and put the long glass to his eye.

At once the magical properties of the spyglass were apparent, for the glass had the power to pierce obscurity. Objects could be seen, even on that moonless night, that never otherwise would have shown, no matter how powerful a pair of field glasses had been used.

Chris, slowly examining, now understood how Claggett Chew's house had originally looked. A road lay at the foot of the hill where they stood. It was the one he and his parents had driven down. It ran north and south, and to his left, he imagined, it eventually led to Riveridge. Behind him somewhere flowed the Shenandoah, and slipping down toward it, past Chew's buildings, was Dragon Run.

Chris could see the big waterfall that he had seen in his own century, a short time before. Looking down at the house, the boy noticed a lane going to it from the road, ending near the front door. This entrance was placed between two windows in the main block of the house. The top of a giant stone chimney rose between the house and a long wing that stretched off to the right. The addition had several windows both upstairs and down; in the lower floor, two windows lay on either side of a wide barnlike door. Quite evidently wagons were expected to drive up to this entry.

At the back of the house Chris could just see a shedlike structure. This was what gave the buildings their L shape. Chris soon realized that the hill on which they stood was not high enough to enable them to look over the top of the pirate's house into the courtyard beyond. He handed the glass to his master with a sigh of annoyance.

"No good, sir," he said. "This hill isn't high enough. We just miss being able to see the fires and the crowd, whoever they are. You try."

Mr. Wicker took the glass and slowly went over the land and buildings. All at once he gave a quiet exclamation.

"Ah! There! Here is something I had not expected. Here, Christopher. Do you confirm what I see — quickly — there at the first window upstairs in the long wing."

Chris snatched the glass and looked hastily through it, directing it at the window described. Sure enough, he faintly saw what had caught his master's attention.

The window was the one nearest the chimney in the long wing to the right, and standing at it could be seen the sorrowing figure of a boy. He was leaning his forehead against the coolness of the panes, staring out into the night. The young face had character and a strange distinction; a curious dignity was there, for all its youth, and aloofness wrapped it round.

"I see him, sir!" Chris cried in his natural tone of voice, in his excitement. "It's a boy! Has Chew a son, do you think? Or could it be — "

"Yes, a prisoner, far more likely," murmured the magician. "But quick! Lie flat, my boy! You have forgotten that Chew also has great magical powers! Your voice broke the air, and while he may not see us, he has now guessed that there is an unusual presence near. See — there he is!"

Raising his head from where he had thrown himself flat on the dewy grass, Chris, taking the glass again, could see the door of Chew's house flung wide. In the yellow oblong of light the great bulk of the man was unmistakable. His closely shaven

68

head and white, colorless face seemed to possess an evil glint of their own in the night. The humped, cringing figure scuttling after him, rubbing his nasty hands and darting glances to right and left, could only be one man: Simon Gosler, Claggett Chew's right-hand man, miser and humpback. Simon Gosler came out from behind his master, holding up a lantern and swinging it here and there. The bands of light from it touched the sinister face of Claggett Chew. The lank mustache drooped over the cruel mouth; the cold eyes looked venomously on all sides, and the restless, powerful hands, clawed by the lantern light, clenched their strong fingers on the handle of his plaited leather whip.

Chris felt his heart beating clumsily at the sight of his ancient enemy, and then he thought to look up at the window where he had seen the young boy.

The child was standing very straight at the window now, looking down at the two fearsome men as they hunted about, with no trace of fear, only an astonishing and admirable disdain.

"Well! Who does he think he is!" Chris thought to himself. "He doesn't seem frightened of either of those two — he can't know them very well, or what they are capable of!"

For some time the two men cast about for intruders that Claggett Chew's quick ultrasensitive nerves had told him were in the vicinity. Finding nothing, and seeing no one, they at last went back inside the house, Simon Gosler limping up the steps on his peg leg.

"Simon Gosler doesn't bother to pretend he's blind, any more, sir!" Chris whispered. "He doesn't even wear his two black eye patches."

"No — there is no one to beg from out here, you see," came Mr. Wicker's low reply. "Let us wait a while until their fears are stilled, and then we must be on our way. I am afraid Chew is always aware of me, as I am of him. Our mutual dislike creates a very disturbing reaction in the air."

"The boy — " Chris whispered again, " — there's something

about him. Who is he, have you any idea, sir?"

"Ah! Perhaps that is one of the things we are here to find out, Christopher! He interests me too. I almost fancy I have seen that face before. But it belonged to a woman, when I saw it last — Now who could that have been?" Mr. Wicker's voice trailed into silence.

"May I change myself into a fly and go and look in the window, sir?" Chris pleaded.

"If you wish, Christopher," came the subdued words, "but if you become a fly, look out for bats! And," he added hastily, "do not stay too long, for Claggett Chew may, even so, be aware of a stranger's presence. Go and look, then, and satisfy your curiosity, and return."

"Yes, sir. I'll be careful." Chris had barely let the words pass his lips, when a fly buzzed past the ear of the magician, who smiled to himself in the dark as it soared away.

The fly flew to the lighted window to the right of the front door, and arriving at the bright panes, kept to a sliver of shadow and peered inside.

It was Claggett Chew's sitting room, on the other side of the wall from the huge fireplace like the one Chris knew there must also be in the shed, judging by the enormous size of the fieldstone chimney. Of Claggett Chew, however, there was no sign. Perhaps he had gone to bed; perhaps — and the thought held a shiver — he was a-prowl about his grounds in the night.

The two fireplaces must be of equal size, Chris thought. At any rate, the one Chris could see was so wide it was out of proportion to the small size of the room. It took up a good part of the wall space, and was at that moment holding a good blaze. Sitting comfortably in front of it was Simon Gosler, the humpback, his peg leg cocked up on one of the swinging iron pot-hooks, in momentary risk of catching on fire. He held a tankard in one hand, from which he took frequent genial swallows. As Chris looked on, Simon put down the pewter mug, and using both hands, forced the wooden peg off the stump of his leg. Chris guessed what would come, but still he waited to see the miser spread his wrinkled bandanna on the hearthstone, and on to it pour from the hollow of his wooden leg a flood of coins that winked and signaled to their greedy owner. Simon rubbed his unwashed hands with avarice and miserly joy, and gave the peg leg a last shake. A final laggard coin came out reluctantly to roll, twinkling, along the wide floorboards and disappear down a crack with a teasing clink.

With a howl of woe, Simon hopped awkwardly over to apply his eye to the crack, putting himself in a most ridiculous position as he bent over. Chris snickered, feeling an ardent wish take shape in his mind, that he might be behind Simon Gosler to administer a kick where it would do both Simon and himself the most good.

Watching the groaning miser as he scratched at the floor and prodded with his knife blade between the boards, Chris knew with relief that Gosler, at least, would be busy trying to retrieve the coin for some time to come; perhaps for the rest of the night. Returning, Chris took back his own form near the magician.

"No sign of Chew, sir," he murmured, "and Simon Gosler's lost a coin down a crack — he'll be busy until he gets it out, which looks as if it would take him all night." He yawned. "Do we wait here?" he asked.

"For a while," Mr. Wicker replied. "Try to sleep."

It seemed hours later, and was perhaps only a short time,
when Chris felt his master's hand on his shoulder and heard
his voice.

"Come, my boy. It lacks but little until dawn. We must
leave this exposed place before light comes."

The two riders went across fields and through rough-hewn
gates finally regaining the road at a safe distance above Claggett's Chew's house. The sun flowing over the Blue Ridge
mountains caught the far fields, and at last pointed out to them,
with a long gold finger, the friendly roofs and colonnaded
wings of Riveridge.

73

CHAPTER 10

*I*T WAS LATE AFTER-
noon when Chris awoke.
The utter unfamiliarity
of his room and surround-
ings was a shock to him, and for some minutes he looked about
him, wondering where he was.

He lay in a four-poster bed. The arched white muslin tester
above his head was belled with white tassels around its scalloped
edge. The walls of the room were blue, and the chair rail, door,
and skirting board were painted white. There were fresh blue
linen curtains at the windows and but little furniture, only
what was necessary. A chest of drawers, a chair and table, and
a walnut washstand with china basin and matching jug.

Then Chris remembered. He was at Riveridge, in one of
the rooms of the guest wing. He shut his eyes peacefully to
recall their arrival. Even at dawn, Jonah was waiting for them
on the doorstep. Had his father, Uncle Borb, been there, instead of on the way, driving Mrs. Moffit's coach and four, it
would have been Uncle Borb's place to receive them, and he
would have taken great pride in doing so at any hour of the

day or night. But it was Jonah who met them in that chill hour, a groom standing beside him to take their horses to the stable. He gave them both a welcoming smile as he helped them to alight.

"Miz Moffit said to tell you 'welcome,' and ask do I show you to your rooms. Says too, to sleep as long as you want to, and to rest yourselves *plenty*."

Holding a lantern, which was rapidly becoming unncessary as the sun rose, he guided them in blue and gilded light along the colonnade that separated the main house from the guest wing, and leading the way upstairs, had shown Mr. Wicker into the larger of the two bedrooms. This room faced toward the Shenandoah far below, with the Blue Ridge beyond, while two other windows on the side opened on to lawns and their forested edge. Chris had stumbled to bed in the smaller bed-chamber that, with two windows also, looked out over the avenue approach to the house, and to the lawn and wood on the right-hand side.

Fully awake now and rested, Chris found that he had a towering appetite. He thought with regret of Becky Boozer's cooking, and without waiting to dress ran along the hall in his nightshirt to see if Mr. Wicker was awake. Voices in the room reassured him, and on knocking and looking in, he saw a familiar and welcome friend.

Aunt Abby, Uncle Borb's wife and housekeeper at Riveridge, was chatting with Mr. Wicker, who had evidently just finished a hearty meal. As the door opened to disclose an eager-faced boy in a nightshirt, Mr. Wicker's eyes began to sparkle, and Aunt Abby clasped her capable hands in surprise and pleasure.

"Well now! Look who's got himself out of bed so early in

75

the day! If it isn't the very boy who rescued my Susie! Bless
your heart, boy — where you been keepin' yourself all these
long months? Welcome to Riveridge and good afternoon to
you!"

Chris shook her hand warmly and wished his master and
Aunt Abby good afternoon. Then he turned back to the mam-
moth woman.

"You're the very one I wanted to see, Aunt Abby. Is there
anything left in your kitchen for me? I feel as if I hadn't
eaten in a week!"

"Bless my heart an' soul — have to do something 'bout that!"
Aunt Abby exclaimed, and pulling Mr. Wicker's bell, in a
moment saw it answered by a neat young Negress in a sprigged
cotton dress and white turban and apron.

"Selena," Aunt Abby said, "please to clear away Master
William's tray, and bring what's waiting for the young master
on the back of the stove. Tuesday's down there in the kitchen;
she has her eye on it."

Chris could not hold back a smile on hearing his reserved and
respectable friend addressed as "Master William," and then
realized that Aunt Abby had probably known Mr. Wicker
when he was younger, and could not imagine calling him otherwise. He was also amused by the odd name he had heard her
use.

"Tuesday?" he said. "That's somebody, Aunt Abby?"

" 'Course it's somebody, boy! Tuesday's my helper in the
kitchen, and doing right well, too. She was born on a Tuesday,
so 'course she *is* Tuesday."

"Does the idea of dressing appeal to you at all, Christopher?"
Mr. Wicker inquired blandly, and Chris became aware with
a start of his bare feet and tousled hair.

"Oh yes, sir! Sorry sir! So much is going on — I forgot
what I looked like!"

"When you are dressed," Mr. Wicker went on, "your late
lunch, or high tea, or whatever Aunt Abby cares to call it, will
be ready. Why not have it here? There are various things I
wished to say to you."

Chris rushed back to his room, and when he returned in fresh
linen and feeling decidedly better for the cold water he had
splashed in, he found Aunt Abby still standing in front of Mr.

77

Wicker, her arms folded along the top of her apron, and her face grave. A tray with many covered dishes had been placed on a low stool before the fire, and as Chris sat down in front of it, his eyes glistening and his mouth watering, Aunt Abby moved ponderously forward to uncover what lay there and see that he was well served.

Four soft-boiled eggs nestled, whole, in a large blue cup, and melted butter made bright rivulets over their white sides, liberally salted and peppered. A separate plate held crisp home-made sausages and strips of bacon, both sending out their inviting and appetizing smells. Under a silver cover a tall pile of buttered toast made Chris wonder where to start, when he saw beside it a glass bowl filled with honey that he guessed must come from Riveridge beehives. In case he did not care for honey, a second bowl of cherry preserves made the boy lift his eyes with a comical look to the dark gentle face above him.

"I never saw so many good things in my life, Aunt Abby! Everything I like best. I hardly know where to start!" he cried.

Aunt Abby poured out a cup of steaming coffee from a silver coffeepot. Without changing her expression or looking up she commented, "Old Master Moffit once say to Master Alec — that's the Colonel — when he hesitate too long over his food: 'Do not fumble with your food, but with one swift glance choose the best!' That's what the old master say," she said, straightening up to look at Chris with more than a hint of laughter in her dark eyes, "an' it always seem a mighty good rule to me!"

Chris laughed, reaching out to the good things before him, but as he ate, relishing every bite, he noticed that his master's face, as well as Aunt Abby's, was preoccupied and stern. Aunt

78

Abby still stood nearby, waiting either to serve Chris or to be dismissed by Mr. Wicker, when abruptly he spoke, leaning his cheek on his hand.

"We may continue with our conversation, Aunt Abby. Christopher, here, knows as much about it as I do, and is likely to know a great deal more before we discover what it is all about." He looked at the majestic Negress, for so many years an integral part of both the Moffits' household and their lives. Aunt Abby returned his look with understanding and her usual dignified air, and waited. Chris chewed, swallowed, enjoyed his food, but was alert for every word.

"Come, Aunt Abby," Mr. Wicker said at last, as if he had gauged how much he could induce Aunt Abby to say, "what sort of slaves are these that Claggett Chew has working for him? Mrs. Moffit says they would not speak to her — they seemed, well, almost as if blind, deaf, and voiceless."

Chris watched Aunt Abby's face. Before his eyes he saw it freeze into an expression he had never seen on it before, and had

never thought to see. The good-humored, slow-moving woman, nearly as large as Becky but with the dignity of a duchess and the unshakable calm of those who have nothing to lose, upheld by a faith that would never leave them, changed before his eyes to a woman he felt he had never known. Aunt Abby's good staunch face became set, sulky, obstinate, with something shifty in it. Her eyes rolled from side to side as if looking for a quick means of escape; her jaws clenched under the soft cheeks, and at last she looked down at her apron, smoothing out nonexistent wrinkles, over and over with her large work-worn fingers.

"That's right, Master William," she said, "it's like you say — they don't speak, seems like. And they 'pear not to hear, so they tell me." She glanced quickly up at Mr. Wicker, and finding him still waiting for an answer, looked down again. " 'Course, you know how it is, Master William. Aunt Abby's always in the house — mostly in the kitchen. Never *do* have time for much else, seems. Time Uncle Borb and me gets to our cabin's time to sleep. No time for either of us to sit gossiping in the quarters — "

She glanced up once more and appeared to see that something she had been waiting for was in the face of the man confronting her, for at once she dropped the whining, soothing tone she had used. Her shoulders went back, as she was in the habit of carrying them, straight and proud, and her face regained its usual placid expression.

"Anything more Aunt Abby can get for you, Master Christopher?" she asked briskly, and when Chris mumbled a no-thank-you, the big woman swept up the tray and with a low "By your leave, Master William" disappeared out the door. Mr. Wicker shook his head, and got up to kick at a burning log on the fire. He looked down at the blaze, leaning on the mantelpiece. Chris, putting away the stool, admired the face etched so lovingly by the fire, waveringly reflected in the gilt-framed mirror hanging over the fireplace.

"One can never make them talk if they don't want to," Mr. Wicker said slowly. "Aunt Abby surprised me. I thought she would confide in us." He shrugged his shoulders as if dismissing the idea. "Nevertheless, she knows more than she cares to say. Well, my boy," and the fine head lifted with a rapid movement, "let us not sit here indoors, but take a quick turn about this beautiful place before the light goes completely. Then — since I believe she has just arrived — I understand that Mrs. Moffit expects us in her sitting room before supper. In the meantime, let us go out and see the lay of the land."

CHAPTER 11

*R*IVERIDGE, SET ON its high knoll, spread its colonnades and walls parallel to the river below. Chris and Mr. Wicker, going out the door of the guest house, found themselves under the covered way, made graceful by many arches, that led to the main house. They had just left behind them, after a cursory glance, the guests' sitting room, directly under Mr. Wicker's bedroom. This faced, with long French windows, on to the terraced lawn that lay across the whole frontage of the plantation house. Without going into the main building master and pupil walked out to the top terrace, and then down long grassy steps to the garden on a lower slope. There they turned to admire the view and the exterior of the house.

Riveridge had been built some twenty-five years before, around 1770, by Mrs. Moffit's husband. He, an English colonist, had brought his English ideas with him to the new rough land he intended making his home, and with the admirable determination of English settlers of whatever generation, the elder Moffit saw no reason why all the amenities of Georgian civilization should not be set down in the wild country of America. His house, therefore, had been built to the specifications of an English architect, and made with English brick, brought as ballast in the holds of many sailing ships and laboriously hauled from Georgetown by cart. To build anything worth while, in Mr. Moffit's opinion, the best materials must be used together with infinite care, or the result could only be shoddy and not worth the trouble of even beginning it.

So for several years he superintended the building of Riveridge and its gardens, for a fine house was, of course, only well set off if surrounded, as a good jewel in a careful setting, by graceful planting and the brilliance of flowers. Besides, Mrs. Moffit, like most women, insisted on a garden, not only to look at, but so that she could decorate the rooms with the fragrance and color of bouquets.

"If we *must* live in the wilderness, Mr. Moffit," she had said to her husband, addressing him in the formal manner which was customary at that time, "then flowers I must insist upon. I should like my English roses, and tulips from Holland; lilac bushes, and lilies of the vale."

"Anything else, madam?" her husband had inquired drily, for he enjoyed teasing Mrs. Moffit.

"Oh yes, most certainly!" came the expected reply. "Here is my list, Mr. Moffit, and please not to forget the English box — I do not care for the American variety!"

Mr. Moffit, smiling to himself after he had turned away, had winked at his agent, who was soon to sail for England.

"You have heard what the lady said, sir!" he said. "Here is

her list, and pray do not omit the English box, since she does not care for the local variety!"

Mrs. Moffit had bristled, but her eyes had a warm affectionate shine, for she was considerably younger then, and very fond of Mr. Moffit.

"Sir! You do make sport of me I fear! Never mind, so long as my plants come in good order I do not care, for flowers I must have. A house without flowers is a dead and lifeless thing!"

So it had been that a fine double-crescent garden had been

laid out below the house, descending green steps of close-cut grass leading to it. The two half-moons of flowers were backed with high hedges of clipped evergreens, against which the changing color of the borders flared with the passing seasons, and gave a vivid display for the windows of the house, higher up the hill, to look down on. Here Mr. Wicker and Chris stopped to face the building, standing so nobly above them on the well-chosen eminence.

The kitchen wing stood to the left, so that in summer the heat of the fireplace and the smell of cooking should be as far removed as possible from the main body of the house. Over the kitchen were the windows of two of the four bedrooms built there for the house servants. An arched colonnade, similar to that joining the guest wing to the main house, led from the kitchen to the door of the dining room, and gave a covered way for the carrying over of dishes. Chris looked from it to Mr. Wicker.

"What happens in winter, sir?" he asked. "A bit drafty, isn't it?"

"Yes," Mr. Wicker replied, "but winters are rarely hard here, as you know. Although this one seems to be making itself ready sooner than usual — " The magician looked thoughtful. "They undoubtedly have an auxiliary, or second, kitchen in the basement of the main house, Christopher, for use when guests are few. Then, the pantry holds many devices and warmers for reheating food and plates, after they have been brought across from the kitchen-house."

"Seems a lot of extra trouble, sir," the boy suggested, looking up at his master. Mr. Wicker nodded with a faint smile.

"It was — is — I should say, my lad, but you must make allowances for habit and old custom. I am sure that if the cooks of the eighteenth century could know the labor-saving tricks of modern kitchens, they would imagine themselves in a mechanical heaven."

The two, master and pupil, smiled, bridging in their experience two such different and distant times. Chris shook his head, still smiling. Mr. Wicker looked at him with amusement.

"A joke, Christopher?"

"Not really, sir," the boy answered, turning up his laughing face. "I was just thinking that with or without modern con-

86

veniences, the food of this time tastes mighty good to me! Guess I'm getting hungry again."

Mr. Wicker threw up his hands in mock despair. "What a barometer and a judge is the stomach of a healthy boy!" he exclaimed, and they turned back to admiring Riveridge, standing serenely above them.

The house itself formed a solid block of rosy brick. In each of the long walls a center door was flanked by high small-paned windows. One of these doors, the front door, faced the circle of the driveway. Shutters on the windows indicated the main bedrooms, and projecting windows in the attic stood out from the roof on each side of the two massive brick chimneys, rising from the center of the house.

"No waste space," commented Mr. Wicker. "Old Moffit was a careful planner." Surveying the whole spread of the graceful house he said, "What a fine and satisfying thing is a good piece of work, whatever it may be! It took courage and vision, Christopher, to turn what was indeed wilderness into this hospitable and gracious place!" He looked down at his pupil. "You seem to have your mind on other matters?"

Chris came back from where his thoughts had led him. "Yes sir. No sir. I mean, I was listening, and I agree. It *is* a fine house. But what I was wondering — that monster that appeared at Mrs. Moffit's window — do you think it flew, or do you think it could have left any tracks?"

"By my soul, you are the boy for this job!" Mr. Wicker exclaimed with pleasure. "I was quite carried away by the color of the flowers in the garden, and by the impression of Riveridge. It is well that you bring me down to earth, Christopher. You are right — the light is going fast. If we are to look for tracks, we must do so at once, for the wind gives promise of rain, and any marks that might be left could be washed away."

Master and pupil hurried up the grass inclines and hesitated under the long windows of Riveridge, where beds of late flowers ran the length of the house.

"Which do you suppose could be the windows of Mrs. Moffit's room, sir?" Chris asked, looking up at the façade of brick.

"I am not sure. One of those facing this way, I should think," Mr. Wicker replied. "I am afraid we shall have to examine the whole length of these flower beds."

"How would it be to start at the steps under the door, sir, and work toward the far ends? Wouldn't it be quicker that way?"

"Yes, Christopher, it would. I will take the left side, and you take the other. We shall have to hurry, for a storm seems to be brewing. Dusk is coming on us more quickly than it should."

Both bent to their task. The well-tended flower borders showed raked and turned earth between the plants, an ideal soft ground for the retention of a print. It was obvious to both Chris and Mr. Wicker that if any monster had set its feet on the ground in order to look in Mrs. Moffit's window, it would have had to step into the flower beds to do so.

Chris bent low, pushing aside the gray-green leaves of the small yellow and russet chrysanthemums and tall asters that made up the bed. Around him he felt the sudden gusts of the rising storm, and turning to glance over his shoulder, saw fast-scudding clouds piling in ominous black masses over the hills that made the Blue Ridge look somber and forbidding. The

river, seen as it curved out around the base of the gradual rise on which Riveridge was built, looked cold and dull, its pewter surface roughed to inky black by the spurts of wind.

Swinging back to work more quickly, Chris found himself nearly at the end of the flower bed when all at once a stronger gust lifted flowers blown over by the wind. There, held in the springy ground were two prints, deep and clear. Looking at them, Chris felt his hair prickle on his head, and a cold that did not come from the storm gripped his body, so that for a breathless moment he remained rigid, as if frozen, staring down.

89

Mr. Wicker, looking up at that moment, could tell by the boy's arrested attitude that something was amiss. He strode up to stand beside Chris, looking closely at what his pupil had discovered. When he straightened up it was with a set face and a grim expression.

"No need to even look, Christopher. Mrs. Moffit's windows must be directly above us," the magician said.

Chris's teeth seemed to have a tendency to chatter, but he governed them to ask in as firm a voice as he could muster, "What could have made that print, sir?"

Mr. Wicker was some time in replying, looking down at the marks as the wind whipped his coat and the first drops of rain hit, hard and cold.

"They would seem to have been made by something that this part of the country does not possess, Christopher. A panther, and of tremendous size!"

Chris was silent, looking from his master's set face to the marks below. Then he found his voice, but it sounded small and distant.

"But, sir, a panther has four feet. Look! These are the only marks to be seen — and there are only *two* prints here!"

Then the full force of the rain struck at them, lashed down on the sound of a terrifying crash of thunder.

CHAPTER 12

*M*RS. MOFFIT'S SIT-
ting room, on the left of
the front door, was a cozy
place in cold weather.
Smaller than the large drawing room beyond that faced the
view, the sitting room had been wainscotted and painted a
pleasing green. The linen curtains were of an English make to
commemorate the founding of the new country, and their pattern of feathered Indians and branchy flowers and shrubs —
considered in England to be symbolic of a country the designer
had evidently never visited — were of a cheerful claret
red against a white ground. Good furniture brought from
England and warm-colored rugs made it a welcoming room,
and one that Mr. Wicker and Chris were happy to reach when
they had tidied themselves from the wind and the rain.

The slender dark maid Selena showed them in, saying, "Miz
Moffit say she be down directly. Make yourselves to home,"
and withdrew, closing the door behind her.

Outside, rain beat at the windows, but inside, the curtains
were drawn and the fire, surrounded by its well-polished brass

91

accouterments, bridled like a flirtatious young woman. Mr. Wicker went up to the blaze.

"Do not, Christopher," he said, "let slip to Mrs. Moffit what we have just found. It would greatly disturb our hostess, I am sure, to let her know of our frightening discovery."

Chris, busy looking around the room, admiring the candlelight, so different from the stronger glare he had been used to, nodded hard.

"Yes, sir. She was nervous enough without that." He gave a reminiscent shudder. "I don't know how well I'll sleep tonight, myself, sir!"

Mr. Wicker gave his pupil a comforting smile. "Nonsense, my boy! There is no reason to believe that the Thing is in any way interested in looking for *you!* How should it know there are guests in the wing, to begin with?"

Mr. Wicker's voice, however, did not hearten Chris as much as it should have, and the boy remained uncertain. He stood looking at a needlework square, half completed, left lying in a straight-backed chair near the fire, and as he was doing so the door opened quickly and Mrs. Moffit, as lively of step and smiling of face as was her usual wont, came into the room.

"My tardy welcome and greetings to you both!" she said, holding out a small hand to Mr. Wicker, and the other to Chris. "I am, though late in bidding you most welcome to Riveridge, none the less heartily pleased to see you! Your presence gives me a sense of security even greater than I had hoped for." She swirled about the room, her great skirts sweeping after her. "Be seated, gentlemen. I am momentarily expecting your two old friends — my dear Susie and David."

"In this storm, ma'am?" Mr. Wicker inquired. Mrs. Moffit

92

took up her needlework with a chuckle.

"We are countryfolk here, William Wicker! A drop of rain does little to dissuade us. If it did we should never stir out of the house all the winter! No indeed. Susan and David have a good solid coach for weather such as this, and sturdy horses. The roads will be muddy, of course, but they will have made allowances, in case they should get stuck in a rut, and will have started off in good time. There," she cried, springing up from her chair and opening the door before Chris had time to do it for her, "I hear the noise of the wheels even now!"

Standing in the hall, lit by glass-protected candles, she loudly clapped her hands to summon Uncle Borb. He was already on his way and came hurrying forward to open the front door, Jonah following after with a lantern. Aunt Abby brought up the rear, wiping her hands on her apron, her face shining with joy.

"Miss Martha, do you stand behind the door!" cautioned Uncle Borb, wagging his head at his mistress. "Rain and wind mighty powerful tonight; no need for you to get your dress soaking wet as well as young Miss."

"Get along with you, Uncle Borb!" countered Mrs. Moffit, pleasurable excitement flowering in her cheeks like two garden pinks. "Open the door for the young people, my mercy! and stop your fretting about the old. Run along out, Jonah, instead of standing there peering around the door. How do you expect them to be able to see their way in! Out with you with your lantern, and light Miss Susie in!"

There was a sudden chill blast as the wide door was opened, and a confused glimpse of the wet side of a coach and four steaming horses as the glow of the lantern skittered and skipped from place to place. A moment later a laughing young person with rain-dashed skin ran into the house and into her grandmother's arms, the hood of her cloak falling off to disclose her glossy hair curling in the dampness.

"Susie, my pet! So good to see you — how is the baby?" came from Mrs. Moffit, and "Darling Grandmother! Stand out of the draft! He's well — I hope you are?" came from Susan almost in the same breath.

Chris, watching the charming scene in the high-ceilinged hall, the upward curve of white stairs beyond, felt a tug at his heart and wished that his eyes could always hold the sight before him. The loving women, bending toward each other, the happy servants, waiting their turn at greeting, and standing quietly near the door, his hat in his hand, the tall handsome figure of Susan Moffit's husband, David Russell. Chris saw with a start that David was now a man grown. Little more than a year before he had looked such a young boy, but now he had the quiet dignity and strength of a reliable and intelligent man. Chris, glancing sideways to his left, saw the especial look that lay in Mr. Wicker's eyes when they rested on Susan Russell. Chris sighed in himself, but still felt that both Mr. Wicker and Susan were better situated as they were.

Susan had become a beautiful young woman since he had seen her. The next few moments were joyous with greetings on all sides. At last, a little calm descending on the company and smiling Uncle Borb being dispatched for wine with which to keep out the cold and wet of the night, the group went into the sitting room to gather around the fire for a chat before supper.

"I look forward to seeing your baby, Susie," Chris said. "It's

94

hard to believe that you have a son!"

"He's the dearest thing in the world!" Susan cried. "Except for his father, of course, and his great-granny over there. You would love him, Chris, he's so fat and jolly."

"What did you name him?" Mr. Wicker wanted to know. Susan flashed him a look that held much friendship, and also much humor.

"Why — Alexander David, after my father and his. Father would never have forgiven me, I think, if we had not named the baby after him!"

"Humph!" snorted old Mrs. Moffit, taking up her needlework once more, but still gazing happily at Susan. "Men are that vain! Still, Alexander is a good name, and if the lad does half as well with it as my Alec has, he will do it honor."

For a while, and after Uncle Borb had brought in their Madeira, they talked as old friends will of many things. Of the Russells' new house, built of squared logs with clapboard over.

"Only a rough building but very snug," David Russell said. "I did a deal of it myself," he added with a trace of pride in his voice.

Mrs. Moffit, plying her needle, interjected, "No sense in the young things having much of a house — they will have Riveridge any year now, when I have gone on my way."

"Do not say such a thing, Grandmother!" Susan cried, her eyes troubled. "Or you will hurt me deeply. We hope to be all of our lives where we now are!"

"Humph!" came again from Mrs. Moffit, who could not restrain a pleased smile. "Pour me another thimbleful of wine, David, to keep out the cold. I fear that winter is already on the way."

Without warning Susan, her hands busy at some sewing too, flung out a casual phrase.

"How is it, Grandmother, that your neighbor Chew can work his slaves by night? David was riding home from Happy Retreat quite a week or so ago — I did forget to mention it — on a moonlight night, and while crossing over Dragon Run he saw a line of men in the long field behind the house." She looked up at David. "You tell them, dear."

David took up the tale. "Yes. They were working in long lines. You can tell by the rhythm of it," he said. "And if a stranger could not have told by that, sure, he would have known the work song. Not that I could distinguish what they sang, and only one or two voices were singing. They sing in another tongue, you know. Some say, they come from Haiti."

"Haiti?" Mrs. Moffit said carelessly, her needle poised but no longer moving, and her eyes cast down.

"Yes — the West Indian island. Perhaps — and this is rumor too — they are sons of the band of soldiers brought over under the French admiral, the Count d'Estaing." David held up his glass to admire the color of his wine and took a sip. "He brought them over to fight in the Revolution. But if this is so, why do they still use their island tongue?"

"Oh well," Susan entered in, "Chew is not a man Grandmother would ever count among her acquaintances, so who cares about his slaves? If they do not run away from being ill treated and worked at night — and none of them ever have, that I have heard of — it is not anything that we can comment on."

"Who is the Count d'Estaing?" Chris asked. David Russell looked at him in some surprise.

"You do not know his name?" David covered his amazement to concede, "Well, of course you were not born then. The Count d'Estaing brought a group of some eight hundred recruits from Haiti to fight for General Washington. They were a colorful and a brave band, so my father used to tell, for the Frenchman dressed them in blue coats with green lapels and white breeches. Their headgear was ornamented with red, yellow, and white plumes. They fought well, and the Count went back for another three hundred and three, who fought under his command at the Battle of Pensacola." David put down his empty glass. "It is perfectly possible that Chew may have brought these directly from Haiti, for some of us know," he said with the twist of a smile at Mr. Wicker and Chris, and at his wife, "that he had done much sailing in his time."

Mrs. Moffit did not look up. "I will warrant the man is a pirate, and that you all know it, and are keeping it from me!" She shot a knowing glance around at the faces of her guests who looked back at her without blinking. "The man behaves as no decent man would!" Mrs. Moffit went on vehemently. "Not only in his treatment of his slaves. If he is not in actual fact a pirate, then he has the heart and soul — and, Lord save us — the look of one, right enough! He has missed his trade, if he never tried piracy!" Mrs. Moffit asserted, nodding her head so vigorously to accent her words that the ribbons on her cap bobbed and fluttered. She gave a long peal on a silver bell standing on the table beside her, and when Uncle Borb appeared she looked up half annoyed and half amused.

"We will have supper now, Uncle Borb, and I hope it is good. For we need some tasty victuals on a night like this to drive the sound of winter out of our ears, and — " she made a grimace, " — take the taste of that odious man's name out of our mouths!" She rose, with a rustle of silk. "Mr. Wicker! Your arm, sir! Shall we go?"

As she led the way Chris made so bold as to offer his arm to Susan, who took it with a mischievous smile. The company put on more cheerful faces and moved out toward the candlelight of the dining room.

CHAPTER 13

*URING THE FOL-*lowing days Chris, his re-membrance of magic re-stored to him by Mr. Wicker, practised all the tricks and changes that he had learned so well over two previous years. Most of every day he and his master would work over the perfecting of these difficult feats in the guests' sitting room in their wing, relieved as the days and nights passed that there had been no recurrence of the monster's presence anywhere about Riveridge.

Chris, standing beside Mr. Wicker, would practise for an hour at a time with the magic rope, throwing it out into the middle air of the room and drawing with it one of the shapes the magic coils could take. Flicking it well out, with rapid turns Chris could transform the innocent-looking length of cord into a rowboat, its sides not only filled in tightly by the magic rope so that it was a solid and navigable craft, but at a further touch from Chris the two ends that dangled on either side would change themselves into oars. And the incredible dinghy could dart over the water with enormous speed.

Or there was the fashioning with the rope of various animal shapes: a camel, a huge beaky eagle, or an elephant. In this last case the two rope ends became the trunk and tail of the pachyderm. Chris, completing the gestures that made the rope into the magic flying eagle, looked at the bird, tranquil in mid-air in the room, with a doubtful expression.

"I wonder if that eagle will ever fly as well again, after being an air lift for Becky," he commented to Mr. Wicker. "Man! I never thought even a magic bird could carry Becky! I'll not forget that night in a hurry!"

"The fact that it could safely carry you and Becky proves that it is magic, does it not, Christopher?" his master replied in a dry tone. Chris laughed.

"I guess it does! That must make it certain, sir! Now," he suggested, "may I try that change into the design of the carpet, sir, or on the curtain?"

"Certainly, Christopher. You seem to have regained excellent mastery over the rope and all its changes. Very well, then. Concentrate on the part of the pattern you wish to be. Repeat in yourself the words of the incantation — no — harder. You are not yet lost in it — there you go — "

And there, indeed, Chris did go. The old familiar humming began in his head as he repeated the magic words and formula in his mind. The dizzy, swimming sensation grew until he felt sick and faint, but he persevered to the end of the words, concentrating the while on a small part of the design in the curtains. With the well-remembered jolt, Chris felt rather cheerful and limp, and at the same time, somewhat angular. Sure enough, he realized that he was a part of the red design in one of the curtains hanging at the front windows of the sitting room. He decided, speechless though he had to be, that he must have made a successful change, for after examining the carpet carefully, Mr. Wicker had to give close scrutiny to the curtains to discover where his apt pupil had disguised himself. When at last the keen-eyed man had found, by a tiny flaw, where Chris was, he gave an exclamation of delight.

"Bravo, Christopher! This is your best change yet! The years and your faithful practice have given you as much perfection as I could hope for in this intricate change. I hardly think that even Claggett Chew could discover you, you are so well hidden. The sharp edge of the design is followed to a nicety, and the color — against the light, it is impossible to tell the difference! The texture of the cloth, too — you hang limp, well woven; in short, I could not have done better myself. Come back now, Christopher, and let us go outside, for I have a new bit of magic for you to try."

Going out into the wood near the guest wing, Mr. Wicker looked up at the trees as they walked away from the house.

"It is time that you went to observe, yourself unseen, what goes on at Claggett Chew's, and to try to discover who the boy is. Although we can, this very afternoon, see what we can see in the silver pitcher. You may remember it. But first," the magician said, coming to a halt near a maple tree, "I have here a phial it may be wise for you to use."

"What is it, sir?" Chris wanted to know, eying the greenish liquid that Mr. Wicker held in a glass phial in his hand.

"This," his master said, holding up the small container between finger and thumb, "is a magical juice compounded of maple essence, and some of the properties of the pine."

"Maple syrup, sir?" Chris asked, brightening.

Mr. Wicker's eyes mirrored his inner amusement. "Something of that sort, but differently distilled," he said. "It has the qualities added of the tenacious sap of the pine."

"Quite a combination," Chris remarked, not too eagerly, wondering what was to come next and hoping the liquid tasted good. "What does it do for me, sir?"

"It turns you, joined with certain incantations you have not yet learned, into as good a maple leaf as anyone could expect. From the high vantage point you can thus gain, you should be able to take in all that goes on below," explained Mr. Wicker.

"What a wonderful idea!" Chris cried. "What are the words, sir?"

"Here they are. Let us begin — "

It was not long before Chris, used to magic formulas now, was word-perfect in the form for change, and — even more important — for his return to his own shape. Repeating the words a final time for his master and then drinking down the liquid from the phial, he kept his eye on the twig he intended to hang on. Chris found himself, after a jolt and a billowy feeling, quite high and light, on the very twig of the maple tree that he had picked out.

"Better and better, my boy!" Mr. Wicker declared from the ground, his upturned face alight with enthusiasm. "What a pity we cannot converse! You did that splendidly. I am proud of you. Come back now, and we shall try it once more to be sure."

The day's work had been a satisfactory one, and master and pupil went back well pleased to the sitting room in the guest wing. Chris, though tired, was curious.

"You said we could see something in the silver pitcher, sir," he reminded his friend. "What did you have in mind?"

Mr. Wicker rubbed his long fingers together thoughtfully, and looked over to a traveling chest that stood in one corner.

"You may remember the first day you came back in Time, Christopher," he began. "You were worried about your mother, who was very ill."

"I do indeed, sir!" Chris replied with fervor.

"In order to let you see that all would be well, I employed magic to enable you to see how she was, and you saw for your-self — and heard — that she would soon be herself again."

"Yes sir! I shall never forget that moment, sir!" Chris took up eagerly. "I remember that you told me that to look in a crystal ball for events past, present, or in the future, was quite — well — old hat." Mr. Wicker smiled. "You proved to me that almost any shiny surface would do. You used the side of the silver water pitcher you had on your table."

Mr. Wicker nodded as he sat by the fire, his legs stretched out and his fingertips together.

"Quite right, Christopher, I did. In case we were not favored with anything as useful for the purpose here, I even brought it with me." He made a gesture. "Be so kind as to open the chest over there, my lad, and let us see what we can see of the young boy's past, in the pitcher's silver sides. I am quite interested," Mr. Wicker said in a thoughtful tone, "at how he came to be there, for he seems to be no son of Clagget Chew. There," he said, when Chris had placed the graceful pitcher on a table by his master, "draw up that stool, my boy, and be alert. We shall see what can be discovered about that serious little boy, and who it is he so much resembles," said the magician.

CHAPTER 14

HE SILVER PITCHER with its smooth round sides stood between the man and the boy who looked at it intently. As on an earlier occasion, Chris gazed at the highly polished side of the pitcher. He sat there still and silent and once more began to lose all sense of where he was. The pleasant sitting room with its fire faded from his attention and the gloss on the side of the pitcher absorbed all his thought and sight.

In a moment the convex curve began to mist over, as if an invisible person were breathing on it. Imperceptibly the mist cleared away and a gray stone building in a city came to view. One window in the building grew larger, seeming to come closer, until the two watchers were able to see beyond the panes into a sparsely furnished room.

As if they hovered outside the very window sill, Mr. Wicker and Chris looked on as a small boy came into sight. He was a happy child, whistling to many-colored birds that hung in cages near the window and around the room. The child, perhaps three or four years old, ran gaily about, talking and singing to his pets, and in a short while took up a length of charcoal and a piece of paper, to try to draw his favorites. This occupation was interrupted by the abrupt opening of a door, evidently well bolted and locked, for a turnkey came in holding a large key in one hand, with many more hanging at his waist. He ushered in a caped man and two followers, who carried between them a large wicker clothesbasket. Waiting until the door of the room was securely shut against prying eyes, the caped gentleman counted out several gold pieces into the hand of the jailer, for so he seemed to be, and tore away the linen that was heaped in the basket.

To the amazement of the two onlookers, another small boy was disclosed lying under the clothes. He was helped out, and was seen to be of the same age, height, and coloring as the first child. There was, however, an important difference between the two children, for while the first was lighthearted and smiling, the second was not so at all, and looked about him fearfully, and at the birds in their cages without interest.

By the motions, for they were too far beyond the window to hear any echo of voices, the two watchers in the Riveridge guest wing understood from the gestures of the caped man that the first child was told to get into the basket. The man laid a finger on his lips as he bent over the boy, to caution him to silence. The bewildered child stretched his hands out to his birds. The caped man said something that soothed the little captive, for he sank back in the basket quietly and with a good grace. The linen clothes were heaped over him, the two bearers picked up the basket, and the jailer let them out, the key to the door ready in his hand to lock up a new and different prisoner. The picture faded upon the sad figure of the new little boy looking about him at the strange room and the many caged birds, prisoners as he was.

"What does it mean, sir?" Chris breathed, not taking his eyes from the silver sides of the pitcher. "The costumes were of this time, only fancier. Who was the boy they took?"

"If I am not mistaken," Mr. Wicker replied softly, "we have just seen the escape of the son of the King of France, Louis the

Sixteenth, from the Temple, the prison in Paris where he and all his family were imprisoned."

"Louis the Sixteenth and Marie Antoinette, who were beheaded in the French Revolution?" Chris queried.

"The very same — the parents of that boy," Mr. Wicker replied.

"That makes the little prisoner Louis the Seventeenth then," Chris said, "wherever he is."

"Yes, my boy. Be quiet. The pitcher is misting over once more —"

The scene that then disclosed itself was of a busy seafaring town.

"That looks like the town of Nantes," Mr. Wicker said, barely audible.

The scene narrowed itself to a prosperous house, and to the garden enclosed by the walls of the house, where a naval officer in the uniform of a French admiral of the period, was following with his eyes the same small boy who had been a prisoner,

as he played on the lawn. The child was unobtrusively watched by two Negroes who stood at a little distance. The child, though obviously a few years older now, was still pursuing his original interest and was following the flight of birds nearby, attempting to coax them to the grass with seeds and crumbs. When tired of this he ran to his dark guardians to demand charcoal and paper, and with considerable skill for so young a child, with quick strokes, caught very passably the character of the birds darting near him.

At a signal from the admiral, the two Negroes withdrew,

leaving the man and the little boy alone. Calling the child to him, the admiral sat down on a bench under a shady tree. Holding the laughing boy close to his knees, the gravity of his expression drove the smiles from the young face before him.

Speaking in French the admiral commanded: "Hold up thy hand!"

The little boy, sensing a moment of importance, drew himself up and held up his small hand, blackened at the fingertips with the charcoal stick he had been using.

"Jean-Jacques," said the admiral, "do thou repeat to me once more thy solemn vow. Once a year must I demand it of thee so that thou shalt remember it well, for thou art young, and the memory of childhood slight."

The child looked up at the big man with affection and confidence.

"My father," he said, "I do not forget, but I shall repeat my vow for thee. For I well know that thou art a second father for me, and not my own, whom I remember now but dimly."

Standing straight and proud, his short hair cut above his eyes across his forehead, he began: "I do most solemnly swear, on penalty of my life, that I shall never divulge who I am, nor what my birth. This do I most solemnly swear," the child ended, and then, dropping his hand and standing on tiptoe, he put his small hands about the admiral's neck to whisper in his ear. "Yet thou knowest, and I know, that I am the King of France, and the son of a king, no matter what I swear. Is it not so?"

The admiral took the child up on to his knees and looked at him sadly, and with some uneasiness.

"Yes, Jean-Jacques, it is indeed so. But thy life would be

110

forfeit, as would be mine and that of my family too, and perhaps the lives of countless good citizens ready to acclaim thee, wert thou ever to forget thy vow." He shook his head as if doubting the ability of so young a child to keep such a heavy secret. The child seemed to understand the expression on his adopted father's face, for he put up his hand to pat the big man's cheek with a gesture that was touching in its effort at comfort.

"Fear not, my dear father. I am who I am. I shall not forget, nor shall I ever be made to forget. Be of good heart," he said with a smile. The man, however, was not reassured, and shook his head again.

"That remains in God's hands, whose ends we must serve," he said. "To be in a safer place, for Nantes is not safe enough in these times of war and revolution for so great a treasure as thou art, I am taking thee from France to my lands in the West Indies. There, thou shalt be out of harm's way, Jean-Jacques, and will be able to draw birds to thy heart's content. There are many tropical birds and beasts that thou hast never seen in those beautiful lands," he said in a more cheerful tone.

The boy smiled up at the anxious face above his. "Thou knowest best, Father. I have every confidence," and he got down from his perch to run after a crow that had walked almost to the feet of the two during their conversation. The crow, looking over its somber shoulder at the child, flapped away and disappeared in the direction of the harbor.

The scene became foggy and vanished.

"Whew!" Chris murmured. "Thank goodness I have French at school or I should never have known what they were talking about! Do you suppose we shall see more?"

"It appears so," Mr. Wicker said, "for see — another scene."

111

When the picture had clarified itself, Chris and Mr. Wicker, leaning forward to miss nothing, saw a tropical shore and a white beach, backed by the brilliance of jungle trees and flowers. Some distance away on a rise of ground could be seen the roof of a house.

From out of a green pathway on the white empty beach, the boy Jean-Jacques emerged, to begin the stalking of sea birds as they ran at the edge of the water. Over the horizon, unnoticed by the child, appeared the sails of a ship, making headway toward the land with a following wind. Chris drew in his breath sharply.

"Look sir!" he whispered. "Black sails! It can only be the *Black Vulture*, Claggett Chew's pirate ship!"

Mr. Wicker made no reply, and the two, watching, saw not only the black sails of the ship approach, but the black wings of a large crow, looking considerably out of place in that tropical setting. It came flying out from the ship to circle the boy as he moved on the beach. Chris again could not hold back an exclamation.

"Sir! That crow! There was one near the boy when he made his vow — could it be Claggett Chew? He once changed himself to a hawk, that I remember only too well!"

Mr. Wicker's voice was serious, but with an undertone of excitement.

"I am afraid so, Christopher. His magic powers are remarkable, as we both know."

The eyes of the boy and the man did not leave the scene so clearly shown before them as they spoke. Far too soon, it seemed to the two onlookers, the great black-winged ship was anchored close inshore, hidden from the house by a turn of the land. A longboat put off, and in no time had been beached near where the boy stood watching with an innocent lack of fear.

A humpbacked, peg-legged cripple in greasy black clothes and with lank untended hair was recognized at once by Chris and Mr. Wicker as Simon Gosler. This evil individual grinned a snaggle-toothed grin of greed and triumph as he directed two

men toward the boy. These two ruffians, one carrying a heavy cape, advanced on the child, who, unsuspecting, stood awaiting them. With a quick movement the foremost sailor flung the cape over the boy, who fell to the sand, tangled in its folds. The two then seized the now struggling captive and hurriedly carried their prize through the surf to the longboat. Even as they pushed the craft off from the shallow water near the beach, two frantic Negroes raced out of the jungle to the edge of the water. One even threw himself into the sea, though unable to swim, in an attempt to rescue his charge, while the other turned to run back and give the alarm to those in the house.

They were too late, for the black sails of the ship were rapidly hoisted, the anchor raised, and the *Black Vulture*, under her greatest press of canvas, was soon only a dwindling, rocking black speck on a vast and empty sea.

The picture clouded and was blotted out as though by a white sea fog, and Chris and Mr. Wicker each drew a deep breath. Mr. Wicker moved from where he had been sitting, and sat down on the other side of the hearth beside the remnants of the fire in a room now almost entirely dark, saying nothing. The windows were only a little less dark than the room itself, and Chris, still on his stool with his chin in his hands, spoke.

"Now we know what treasure Simon Gosler shared, 'worth a nation's ransom,' " he said. "And how that boy came to be where he is —"

Mr. Wicker's voice came out of the dusk. "And I know now what woman's face it was, that reminded me so strongly of the boy. It was Queen Marie Antoinette herself. I saw her once, driving out of Versailles, when I was younger," he said in a dreamy tone. But sharp as the break of glass his voice cracked out at Chris, "Quick, Christopher! The window!"

There was a sudden brush against the windowpanes, and Chris, jumping up, overturned the stool in his haste to see what it was. He turned slowly around from the window and his face was white in the light of the candle.

"It was a bird against the window, sir!" he cried. "A dark — a black bird!" He looked, terrified, at Mr. Wicker. "It seemed to me, sir," he whispered, "that it was a crow!"

114

CHAPTER 15

W HEN CHRIS HAD SPO-
ken, his face pale with the
knowledge of who had in
reality been spying on him-
self and the magician, Mr. Wicker's first movement was char-
acteristically rapid. Setting down the candle he strode across
to the windows and with brusque motions drew the curtains
close across the panes. Next, lighting the remaining candles in
the room, he returned to pace up and down before the fire.
Chris's eyes followed the neat bent head, the black well-fitting
suit that never seemed gloomy, the cleanly defined features of
the man who had taught him so much. In his own good time,
after much thought and a long silence, Mr. Wicker stopped
his meditative pacing and looked up with the familiar decisive
lift of his head.

"I know now that you were right, my boy," he said. "One
has to be certain — it *could* have been an ordinary bird flying
against the panes." He looked into Chris's anxious eyes. "Your
eyes are keen. What you saw was a crow, as you thought, but
no usual one: it was Claggett Chew." He looked down into

the fire and then off to some far place, beyond Chris's and all average sight. In a moment he went on.

"We are forced ahead, therefore, more quickly than we had intended. There is no time to lose. This very night you must go down to Claggett Chew's house and do your utmost to see if the prisoner there can be freed. For Chew now knows that we have discovered the identity of the boy, and has surmised that we shall act on this knowledge." His look was piercing as he faced the frightened lad standing rigid before him, yet Chris felt a new strength coming to him from the eyes of his friend. "What Claggett Chew does not know, Christopher, and *must* not know, is that you will be near him tonight. You must remain hidden at all costs."

At Chris's stricken face, filled with doubts of his own abilities, and obviously at a loss on where to begin such a frightening assignment, Mr. Wicker took a long step forward to put his hand on his young pupil's shoulder.

"Do not fear, Christopher! Fear itself is your worst enemy! Have faith — for you know much, and you know it well. Besides, you have the subtle but powerful help with you at all times of being an instrument for good, while the fact that Claggett Chew stands for destruction and evil is as though his every weapon was already cracked or rusty. There is always, my boy," said the magician, looking down at the earnest face, "the flaw of weakness in a wrong act. There is always in it the fission that will, in the end, destroy it. Remember that. Now," he said, going with long steps to his locked traveling chest in the corner, "put the bag of magic odds and ends about your neck, for you must be off, and no time lost."

Chris still stood before the fire as if paralyzed, almost hoping

116

that his feet would take root and that he would be unable to move.

"What shape had I better take to get there?" he finally asked. Mr. Wicker did not even turn around, kneeling in front of the chest.

"Tut, tut, my boy! What is this? Consider what part of the world you are in and the answer will present itself. You are on no ship now. No sea bird shape will do. You have been practising all your animate and inanimate changes — as many, that is, as can be done. For magic, as we both know, has its limits like everything else."

As he stood, once more holding a small leather bag in his hands, the boy near him looked him in the face with new determination, all trace of his indecision and nervousness gone.

"I shall be a fox, sir," he announced. "They abound in this country, I hear. May I have the bag now, sir? The sooner I get off the quicker I may be able to get results. As you have often said, 'the element of surprise is a strength in itself.'"

Mr. Wicker's expression eased into a relaxed half-smile. "Now you are my own lad once more, Christopher!" he said, in a tone of deep satisfaction. "Your momentary misgivings did not suit you. Here, wind the magic rope around your waist — you may need it and you may not. And hide the phial of maple liquid, for this I know you can use. Bend your head — there. Now you have your old friend with you — the bag of magical odds and ends that have come in at times so handy, have they not?"

Chris grinned. "That's what's known as the depths of understatement, sir!" he replied. "I'm sure I wouldn't be alive if it hadn't been for this wonderful bag!"

Mr. Wicker's face changed. Now that his pupil was ready to go out on this important reconnaissance, perhaps even he had misgivings.

"Report to me every twelve hours, Christopher," he cautioned. "Otherwise I shall know that something has gone amiss — if I am not able to discover it some other way. For, make no mistake about it, Claggett Chew's magic can cause serious interference with my own."

"The silver pitcher, sir?" Chris asked.

Mr. Wicker shook his head. "The best way I can explain what he can do, my boy, is that in your twentieth-century time, certain foreign countries, objecting to what we broadcast, can 'jam' the air waves and turn our broadcasts into jumbled useless noise. This, in magic, is what Claggett Chew can do with my own. I can usually get the better of him, but he is a powerful enemy, Christopher, as you know only too well, and not to be lightly tampered with."

Chris's head bobbed his solemn agreement. "I know, sir. No need to remind me. And I daresay he still has new tricks up his sleeve that I know nothing about."

Mr. Wicker sighed. "I am afraid so, Christopher. To be on the alert every breathing moment is almost not alert enough. Well — " and he clapped the boy on the shoulder, giving him a heartening smile, " — see what you can discover, and let me know. I shall be waiting to hear." He walked to the sitting-room door, his hand still comfortingly on the young shoulder near his own. "Above all, my boy, take no chances. I only wish I could go in your stead, but two at this game are better than one, and it is wisest for me to remain here to come to your aid if this should be needed."

118

The outer door of the guest wing was reached; Chris stopped and held out his hand.

"I'll go alone from here, Mr. Wicker, sir," he said. "I'll do my best, you know that."

His master nodded, concern in his eyes. "Yes. I know that, Christopher. Now, Godspeed to you! Take care!"

The door shut, and the frigid air of late October struck Chris with its raw blast. The boy hesitated, took a deep breath, and then from the black shadow of the colonnades of Riveridge a red fox trotted quickly in the direction of the wood and of the hidden ways, as the first flakes of an early snow began whirling down the night sky.

Facing the house of its enemy the fox paused, one paw lifted. Something even more unusual than when on the first occasion Chris had seen the pirate's retreat, was going forward. A surge of voices and shrill cries came from the hidden open space within the protecting walls, and a blaze of fires flashed and flapped in the heavily falling snow.

To the left of the buildings a hill rose higher than the house roofs; the ridge appeared to continue for some distance. In spite of the heavy wood densely covering it, Chris hoped that the rise of ground would allow him to see what went on without being dangerously close. At the moment all was effectively hidden from him by the group of the buildings themselves.

Running hard, the limber red animal, its brush blowing out behind it, ran up the hill to wind in and out of thickets and underbrush until it was, Chris judged, far enough past the long shedlike wing at the back of the house to be able to see over.

To his keen disappointment this was not the case. The wood

and shrubs, looped with honeysuckle, green even in the snow, made a hopeless barrier for a fox low to the ground. Inching his way down the incline, therefore, Chris as a fox crept closer to the source of the flames, the hoarse and cutting cries; the welling excitement that was carried on the cold snowy air. Creeping to the edge of the wood, though he saw himself to be only a hundred feet or so from the house, he now realized that the stream, by its angled turn, prevented his getting close enough to the scene he wished so urgently to see.

Sitting on its haunches, the red fox contemplated its next move, grateful that the magic rope and the leather bag of magic "odds and ends" would diminish or hide themselves, according to whatever shape he chose to take.

The long shed, making an intervening wall between Chris and what he wanted to see, ended in a stone chimney only slightly smaller than the vast chimney beyond, rising between the house and the front wing. Near the smaller chimney, which the fox was eying, a small space of eight feet, not more, gave a narrow margin to the bank where the first of the three waterfalls fell with a dull roar. Some sort of dam had once been built to make it, for the ruins of a stone wall could be seen on either side. There the water suddenly smoothed itself glassily before its twelve-foot drop, to continue the stream below. Just at the top of the dam the water made a deep pool, held in by grassy banks on the far side, and on the near side by the roots of tall ancient willows, growing close to the house.

All along the stream, as it passed through the neighboring half-mile pasture, towered a row of willows so old, judging by their heavy trunks and branches, as to have been beside the watercourse many years before Claggett Chew was born.

The fox surveyed all this from the high shadow of the wood. It could catch sight of the leap and play of shadows thrown against the steep bank beyond the waterfall which were not those of firelight alone. Chris became more than ever impatient to see what went on, and with a thrust of inspiration looked at the tree overhanging the falls.

It was an old willow, its branches stretched high up above the chimney and the roof; high enough to afford an unimpeded view of any scene below.

For only a moment did Chris revolve the problem in his mind. The snow had slackened and stopped; a white undisturbed fall rested on every twig and leaf, for many leaves still remained, and the snow on their brilliant yellow or oxblood red the next morning would make, the boy thought, a vivid sight.

Chris debated with himself only a moment more, and then, taking his own shape, with the utmost caution and in the covering of the trees, he drank off the phial of maple liquid while repeating to himself the necessary incantations and fixing his eyes and his attention on a certain topmost branch, well away from all obstructions, at the very top of the willow tree.

There was a lurch and an unsolid, breathless feeling, and the boy who had been only a few moments before a fox on four legs, found himself a leaf hanging on a twig of the willow tree, in possession of a superb view of all that passed below.

The only thing was, that among the thin yellow willow leaves, there hung a lone green maple leaf.

CHAPTER 16

A LARGE SQUARE space lay under his eyes. The house, wing, and addition near him almost enclosed two sides, to his right and going far across to the left. The turning stream formed the limits of the other two sides, along the left side and immediately behind him. What small gaps remained to be filled to create the four walls of the square were effectively done by trees and thick American box, evidently left for that purpose.

It would have been, doubtless, an innocent-enough looking space in daytime; merely a patch of ground. Just then, however, Chris, with a prickling of fear, felt that he must have been transported to Africa.

A huge circle of thirteen fires blazed below him on the snow, leaving little or no space between their urgent flames. What astounded Chris in the wild and tumultuous spectacle beneath him, were the half-naked figures whirling in and out of the fires, weaving and leaping over the sparks in a human chain. They were the mysterious slaves Mrs. Moffit had tried

to speak to, and that David Russell had seen in the distant field. Their dark-skinned bodies moved in and out of the glare of the fires, while the braided cords, beads, feathers and shells with which they were decorated made unpredictable patterns of color. But although they leaped or flung up their arms, gyrated, or swung from side to side, not one man among them uttered a sound, and the eyes of the strange slaves stared sightlessly, like those of blind men.

Chris, uneasy enough at being in a shape to which he had not had enough practice to become accustomed, felt such a

chill invading all his being, as these curiously behaving men
moved in their dance-patterns, that it needed all his concentration to hold to the safety of his disguise. Presently he had time
to be aware that the rhythmic clapping came from a group of
women, sitting cross-legged beyond the fires on the snowy
ground. Their turbans and cotton dresses, once perhaps of
many colors — rose, yellow or blue — were now faded almost
beyond telling what they had once resembled, and hung slackly
on their bodies. Their eyes, too, stared into nothing, and the
frozen ground on which they sat seemed not to make their

flesh colder, or uncomfortable. They sat in a motionless semi-circle with their backs to the shed, some clapping their hands, some drumming on crude drums, but making no outcry and no sound.

"What's the *matter* with these people?" Chris wondered, puzzled and increasingly fearful. As his attention went from face to face, and then to the strangely monotonous leaping and swaying of the half-naked men, his concentration was caught by the central figures.

These were three. The foremost was a gigantic Negro of magnificent proportions and height, standing easily six-feet-six, with a fine muscular physique. The shine of his skin, deep-dark in the firelight, was a contrast to the dulled skins of the dancers and that of the clapping women. This tall figure carried his head well and proudly, and this in itself became not only the sign of a leader but of great strength, for he wore a headdress largely composed of two far-branching horns. These, as big around at their base as a man's arm, tapered as they curved outward, their sharp tips shading from bone-white to black.

Those aren't the horns of any cattle *I've* ever known! Chris thought to himself. Then he continued to examine the face and costume of this extraordinary man.

His features were clear-cut; his eyes of a penetrating power. What little of his hair could be seen was braided and laced with the pointed teeth of a leopard — or so Chris supposed, since bands of leopard skin bound his wrists and were used in the headdress. Feathers and shells sprang from under the great horns; multicolored feathers of no birds Chris knew. A leopard skin covered his back in such a way that the head of the beast fell forward over his chest. A red cloth bound his loins, and

126

strips of the same material held a series of bells around his ankles that carilloned as he moved. In his left hand he held a whisk made from the black mane of a lion. All in all, he was a prideful and an awesome sight, and yet Chris could not find him as frightening as the dancers, or the dim, staring women in their colorless garments.

Beside the big horned man stood an ancient colored woman in a calico dress, her head crowned with many-dyed ostrich plumes. Her wrinkled face had shrunk as age had claimed her for its own, and showed such an expression of venom and evil that Chris felt a shudder strike him as his attention reached her. She followed the whirlings of the dancers with apparent pleasure, mumbling and chewing her old gums — for she did not appear to have a tooth in her head. She held a small bowl heaped with some substance in one hand; the other, restless and swollen-veined with years, twitched at her skirt as if she was afraid some part of it might touch the big man beside her. She shot looks of hatred toward him, frowning, and tossing her head the while, to which the enormous Negro paid not the slightest attention. Behind the old woman stood a pretty young Negress, seemingly not happy to be at the beck and call of the wily evil one before her.

Around them capered a dark-skinned yelling pigmy, teasing, laughing, tweeking the old woman's skirts, trying to steal a kiss from her young attendant's cheek, and making faces as he postured behind the back of the tall Negro, whom he dared not face.

The old woman finally had enough. Without turning, in a dialect that was hard for Chris to understand, she spat at the pigmy:

"Baka! If you not still, old Mamba make you eat *kingolo* root, and sacrifice you to Erzilie-Gé-Rouge, the Red-Eyed One!"

The effect of this on the pigmy was instantaneous. His face became pinched with fear, and he fell forward on all fours in the trampled snow in front of the old woman. She looked down at his groveling form with scorn and sour satisfaction, jerking the hem of her skirt out of the crawling pigmy's beseeching fingers as he beat his head on the snow and howled.

"Non-non! No, Mamba! Priestess of Erzilie-Gé-Rouge, pity thy servant! Mercy — mercy! Sweetest Mamba!"

"How sweet am I, clown Baka?" demanded Mamba. The poor pigmy lifted himself partly off the snow, rolling his eyes as he attempted to save himself by blandishments.

"Sweeter than the milk of new corn kernels, Mamba. Sweeter than sugar cane — " he paused, and his expression changed. "Baka hungers for sugar cane!"

Mamba stamped her foot. "No tell Mamba what Baka hungers for! Tell Mamba how fine is Mamba!"

The pigmy hung his head, abject before the relentless old woman. Then he had an inspiration and looked up desperately.

"Fine enough to be finest priestess of the Big *Ouanga*, the Death-*Ouanga*, now — here! Big Bossal, is Mamba. Borned in Africa. Finest priestess of the Evildoer, red-eyed Erzilie-Gé-Rouge!"

Mamba was satisfied. She nodded her old head. "So! Finer than Agona — " She curved her thumb at the huge man at her side, who neither moved nor spoke. "Is it not so, Baka?"

"Yes — yes!" shrieked the frightened pigmy. "Yes — yes!"

"Agona, priest of Damballa-Oueddo," the old woman

129

sneered, "the One of Light, the One of Goodness. But Mamba is priestess of the Evil One, Erzilie-Gé-Rouge!"

Without warning, for the muscles of his face had not moved by so much as a flicker, a deep gust of sound rolled over the pigmy as the big man spoke. His resonant voice, it seemed to Chris, tore echoes rumbling and shivering from the wooded hill, and drowned out the roar of the waterfall below him.

"Baka! Rise like a man, for so thou art, even small! Come to stand behind Agona, who will let no woman touch thee!"

"Less'n I wants?" cut in the pigmy, with a side glance at the pretty young Negress near Mamba.

"So may it be," Agona said. "Agona — hold it well in thy skull, Baka! — is priest for Damballa-Oueddo, Lord of Heaven, whose foot lies until the end of Time upon the neck of Erzilie-Gé-Rouge, the Evildoer."

The old woman hopped up and down in her rage, hurling imprecations and scornful epithets against the man, who received them as if they were rain upon a mountain.

Into this scene two figures now were added, coming from the main part of the house, from the wide door of the wing across from Chris, and followed by a slave carrying two chairs. The two were Simon Gosler and Claggett Chew, the latter striding forward wrapped in a fur-lined cape, his shaven head bare to the icy air.

Hope he catches his death of cold! Chris thought, and watched as a second slave came out holding two flagons, which he put into the hands of his master and Simon Gosler. Gosler received his with a cackle of glee, tilting the bottle to take a hasty swig of whatever it contained. Claggett Chew, his cruel face immovable, sat down on a platform reached by steps out-

130

side the door of the shed, in profile to Chris, facing the fires and the central figures. The long wall of the shed afforded some protection from the cold, and gave a good view of the ceremony before them. The pirate sat there staring and silent, holding his bottle upon his knee. Then he held up one large brutal hand for silence.

It was immediate. The drums were stilled, the leaping figures frozen to quiet in mid-step. In the blink of an eye, Chris, over-hanging everything, could hear no sound but the cold thunder of the waterfall behind him and the crackle of the fires before him. Slowly Claggett Chew rose, turning to look down at Simon Gosler, who was tipping his bottle to his mouth again in greedy haste.

"Hear all, and all be witness!" Claggett Chew's cold voice filled the stillness. "Simon Gosler and I have placed a bet upon what we are to see —"

131

" — or not see!" cackled the humpback from his chair, wiping his lips with the back of his dirty hand.

" — or not see," Claggett Chew resumed, as though he had not been interrupted. "I say that Agona, being a man, has better magic than Mamba. I have wagered a purse of gold pieces to Simon, here, should Agona fail. If he wins, Agona himself shall have whatever is in my own purse — " and he held up a double purse clasped by a ring. Simon Gosler rubbed his gnarled hands and smiled his ugly snaggle-toothed smile, peering up through the strands of lank hair that fell over his face at the figure of his master, standing so tall above him.

"Eh, so it is!" he agreed cheerfully, and then a dubious look brushed his smile away. "Only — what sort of magic will they use, eh cap'n?" he whined distrustfully. "Not harmful to our prize, eh? No hocus-pocus, eh?"

Claggett Chew threw himself down into his chair, drawing close the folds of his cape, and stretching his booted legs in front of him.

"Stop whining. Is the bet on, or no?"

Simon, thinking over the prospect of a bag swollen with gold pieces, rubbed his hands and grinned slyly.

"Aye, cap'n! The bet's on, right enough. Whatever you wish! Whatever you wish!"

"Very well, begin!" Chew called out to the central figures, disregarding, as if they had not been there, the vacant-eyed women, the interrupted dancers. "Let us see which has the strongest voodoo — Agona's Damballa-Oueddo, or that of the Red-Eyed One! Begin the *ouanga!*"

"Mamba shall win! Mamba shall win!" chuckled Simon Gosler, clutching his greasy clothes about him and taking many a sip from his bottle to keep out the damp cold. "I believe none of it," he muttered. "They will never do anything. 'Tis like an old wives' tale — all mumble-jumble and nothing but air in the end!"

"Bring out the boy!" roared Claggett Chew to the two slaves who had returned to the long wing, and were standing by the wide barnlike door awaiting their master's orders.

"Then bring out my cat too!" screamed the excited hunchback.

To Chris's horror, from the black gaping maw of the door, a tiny figure emerged walking proudly between the two slaves, each of whom held one of his small arms. They were dressed, as was the boy, in worn blue cotton breeches, knotted tightly at the knee over bare legs, and with ragged shirts. The only difference was that the two men had machete knives stuck into the belts of their trousers.

What in the world is going to happen now? Chris wondered, straining to miss nothing across the snow, the many fires and the twisting smoke, the confusion of the leaping men, to follow every movement of the young king.

The child held himself as a king should. He did not fling back his body, to defer the moment nor resist, neither did he let his head droop nor his step falter. That his face was pale was because he was human, and only eight years old. He walked manfully between his two jailers — he who had known but little else all of his few years of life — and when he came opposite to the giant Agona he looked up with such challenge in his bearing that there was an answering flash of sympathy and admiration in the eyes of the horn-headed Negro, gazing down.

133

Under the fingers of the women the clapping and the drumming rose higher and stronger, pounding along the night air until it sounded out in long rolling waves. Snow, delicately poised on the leaves of the willow trees, fell to the ground, disturbed by the vibration of the noise.

The big man looked from his height down to the child, and the old woman, sneering and confident of her power, rasped out: "What thee say, boy? Thy last word?"

Jean-Jacques bore his heritage and the name of his adopted father with honor. He never took his eyes from the tall man above him, whose somber glance was locked with his own. His thin child's French piped clear as a flute, and at a gesture from Mamba, the drums fell silent.

"Agona," spoke up the boy, raising his voice as if in an effort to send it as high as the distant ears of the man so far above him, "Agona, thou seems to me to be a king. A king without a land, without a people, and without a throne. And thou art a man. I say to thee: by God's dear grace, so should another be!" Whereupon he folded his arms, set free by the two slaves, and stood firmly on his short legs, looking defiantly into the face of the towering man.

Agona, for a long moment, fought to suppress an expression which Chris as eagerly tried to read. It appeared to be a mixture of sorrow, anger, remembrance, and a relentless desire for revenge, but none of it was directed against the child facing him. Against whom, it would have been hard to say.

Just then the drums took up their rising, quickened beat, and from the square black mouth of the distant open door, centered in the long wing, there walked a large, proud, and leisurely yellow cat.

134

CHAPTER 17

A LOW CHAIR WAS placed for Mamba on which she sat with the regal stateliness of someone of overwhelming importance. Baka the pigmy, and the young girl, attended her; the two slaves who had brought out Jean-Jacques stood to the right on either side of the little boy, while Agona, magnificent in his disdain, watched the proceedings with an inscrutable face.

The old woman in her calico dress and slippers of sisal sat as rigid as a queen. In one hand she held a calabash, ornamented with painted signs and symbols, rattling with strings of vari-colored beads. In the other hand she held a bell. About her neck were hung necklaces of adder's vertebrae which chatted ominously together when she moved. Her feathered headdress was startling in its color above the dark thousand-wrinkled face. She sat still while the young Negress, Baka, and the two slaves chanted and wailed. All at once, Mamba rose from the chair to begin a pacing that became quicker, until she writhed and turned. The chanting stopped and Mamba's voice, as strong as that of a young woman's, came out high and loud.

"*Hé! Hé!* Erzilie-Gé-Rouge — it is I! *Hé! Hé!* It is I — Erzilie-Gé-Rouge!"

Mamba no longer seemed to be Mamba, for all her gestures were strong; her ancient body was shaken and twisted, bent and pulled upright, as if in the grip of powerful hands.

"It is I — Erzilie-Gé-Rouge!" she shrieked, and placing the bell and calabash on the chair as if on an altar, she took the hand of the young Negress and of the wincing Baka on her other side. They began a complicated ritual of dance steps, pivoting first to the left, then to the right, prancing, bowing. All three appeared at last to be lost in the rhythm of the drums, rising and falling in their pounding, the deep-throated wail of the slaves, and of their own motions.

The young woman broke away at last to offer Mamba liquid in a bowl, chanting, "Orgeat for Erzilie-Gé-Rouge! Orange-flower water for the Red-Eyed One!"

Mamba drank, and abruptly whirled. Seizing ash from the nearest fire and her calabash from the chair, with gestures and prancings, she advanced to stand before Jean-Jacques. The child did not move, although his eyes grew bigger and he seemed to be forcing his legs into the ground to hold them there.

Chris, straining to lose nothing that the scene below could bring him, decided that the unintelligible words Mamba was using were by no means the gibberish they seemed to be, but were ritual phrases in Haitian, or the African of her own tribe. Her voice keened like that of an animal at the moon, making Chris shiver within himself as she sifted ashes on the boy's head.

"I, Erzilie-Gé-Rouge, do make flesh dust!" Motioning with

136

her hand, stained gray as bones with wood ash, she summoned the girl, who shrinkingly and hesitantly took up and brought to the priestess a beaker made from a human skull.

"Drink!" screamed Mamba, seizing the skull and thrusting it at the boy, who would have recoiled but was held fast by the two slaves. "Juice of *kingolo* — drink — drink! Death is no death with *kingolo!* Taste! Taste for Erzilie-Gé-Rouge!"

As Jean-Jacques still hesitated, at a shrieking signal from Mamba, a brown thick-bodied snake uncoiled itself from around her neck where it had lain like a rusty collar, and directed its weaving triangular head, symbol of poison, at the boy.

"See!" cried Mamba, as the snake stiffened a few inches from the blanched face of the child, "Erzilie's own is here! Choose *kingolo*, the living death! Move as a zombie, soulless and heartless, mindless and heedless, or choose the twisting death of

Erzilie-Gé-Rouge! Choose! Choose!"

The boy, his face the color of a fish's belly, could not move. In that horrifying second, the great hand of Agona flashed out, tearing the snake from the neck of the old woman, and with a movement too fast for the eye to follow he had torn off the head of the reptile, tossed it into the closest fire and flung the writhing body that takes so long to die at the feet of its enraged owner. A second sudden sweep came from the huge-horned figure as Agona struck the skull with its deadly drink from Mamba's hand, even as the terrified child was being forced to put out its hands to take the loathsome cup. Agona's deep voice sounded across the flames, the silent dancers, the women at the drums.

"Neither snake nor *kingolo* is magic! He shall not become a zombie for Erzilie-Gé-Rouge! Agona, Watusi warrior, priest of Damballa-Oueddo, shall prevent it! And all shall see the true magic of Damballa-Oueddo, Lord of Light!" came the rolling words.

Mamba, beside herself with rage, chattered and screamed. Words could finally be understood, together with her gestures at Jean-Jacques.

"See! He shake, he tremble! The cold of death touch he bones! The ash from which he come, call he back! Erzilie still queen!"

With a push, the now infuriated Agona thrust the old woman back until she fell into her chair aghast. Grasping a bottle where it had been ready to his hand in the snow, Agona poured onto the head of the white and staggering boy a clear liquid which the moving air soon told Chris was rum. Agona then took from a colored bowl wheat flour with which he traced

138

on the ground a large circle, and then a series of designs sacred to Damballa-Oueddo. Prostrating himself, he kissed the symbols in a gesture of humility, wiping the muddy snow from his lips. At a wave of his arm, drums rolled louder than ever and Agona began his own dance, leaping in and out of the thirteen fires, circling the ritual symbols of his god, and whirling around the child, who seemed on the verge of fainting.

The wild horned figure, overleaping the fires to the rhythmic throb of the drums deep, light, and high in tone, was unforgettable. As the dance drew to a close, Agona gave a high catlike cry, and the yellow cat that had sauntered from the wing came forward, tail flicking, eyes green slits.

It threaded its way among the zombies, cross-legged now on the snow, rocking from side to side; past the women and their sightless, changeless faces, the beat and thunder of the drums. With a dash, in answer to Agona's repeated cat cries, the great yellow beast came to the feet of the horned priest, whose dark skin glistened with sweat, a frenzy of effort upon him.

Kneeling at the base of the wheat-flour symbols of Damballa-Oueddo, one of Agona's powerful arms reached out to hold the boy and force him to his knees. With the other he held the cat, which crouched, spitting and hissing softly, but did not struggle. To one of the slaves Agona thundered "Bring the bowl!" and as the man raced away, the giant Negro began to chant, to the accompaniment of the drums.

"Papa Legba, guardian of the heavenly gate, open it that Damballa-Oueddo may hear his servant! Dragon, dragon underground, dragon of the forest that neither grows nor dies, guardian of lost souls that wander far from home — hear thou thy servant, the priest and warrior Agona!"

Carried away by the compelling voice of the big man and by their own emotions, the slaves who surrounded Mamba, and even Mamba herself, screamed and wailed in terror and abasement. The slave came hurriedly back carefully carrying a basin whose lip was stained with liquid of too red a color.

Chris felt sick, and clung harder than ever to his disguise and his concentration on it. The liquid was, without any doubt, nothing less than blood. Over the kneeling giant, the cat, and the boy wove the coiling filmy sheets of smoke, flashes of spark and fire, and behind and around them all spread the white trampled snow, the frozen stillness of trees and air.

Agona spoke again, but this time in a low monotone that made his listeners sleepy. It affected both the cat and the child, for as he spoke, turning first to the cat and then to the boy, the eyes of animal and human glazed, and although they stared fixedly at one another it was plain that a deep inner change was taking place in each, and that they were no longer aware of where they were nor why, neither sensible to the cold nor the fire's heat.

"Jack-cat," purred Agona, with catlike noises rumbling in his throat, the shadow of the long pointed horns darting like something alive in the firelight, "cat, look thou well and deeply in the eyes of this boy." Throwing his head back he shouted, "Damballa-Oueddo! Hear thou, and see!" Calling out once more to the slave, who stood quaking as he held the bowl of blood in his hands, "Pour the offering to Damballa-Oueddo! Pour!"

Little by little the red blood trickled to the ground between the motionless cat and the child, who stared fixedly at one another.

140

"Boy — boy," came Agona's voice, "by the wish of Damballa-Oueddo be thou the cat!"

Pulling strips of red cloth like ribbons from among those that bound his ankles, Agona decorated the heads and necks of the now absolutely still pair. The second slave went into the wing of the house and returned with a dead white dove, blood on its neck in echo of the crimson patch of blood upon the snow, and with the dove's blood Agona marked the foreheads of animal and child.

The first slave finished the slow pouring of the blood upon the ground, and at a motion from Agona all drums ceased. So intent was he on the ceremony, Chris thought that the waterfall must have stopped too, for a silence seemed to stun the air, taking from it all sound except Agona's voice.

"Boy, be thou cat; cat, be thou one with boy! Damballa-Oueddo, save this soul from Erzilie-Gé-Rouge, the Evil One, the Evil-doer!"

And as he spoke, the cat, under Agona's big hand, appeared to crouch and then, imperceptibly, to shrink, while the boy, grotesque as he looked, hung about with red ribbons of cloth, his forehead smeared with the white dove's blood, grew smaller, smaller, shrank into his clothes, until with a start of horror Chris was aware below him of the square-cut hair growing tawny, fading to a yellow-orange. The human ears became too small — began to point at their top ends, and a fuzz to cover them. And when, with a convulsive movement, what had been Jean-Jacques struggled out of the constricting clothes, a cat sat there, an overlarge, yellow cat; while of the cat itself there was left nothing more than a little heap of blanched, useless bones.

142

CHAPTER 18

*J*NTO THE HUSH, OF the onlookers' hearts if not in actual fact, came the unprecedented guffaw of Claggett Chew's laughter. It broke the scene with the sound of glass breaking, or the grinding of ice in a muddy river. It was frightening, shocking laughter, unpractised and harsh. Chris, leaf that he temporarily was, shook on the bough to which he must cling by concentration. The Negro figures who had taken part in the fantastic event just disclosed, or who had watched it, hypnotized by what their eyes so evidently found it hard to believe, raised startled heads. With one accord the several dark faces swung from Agona and the yellow cat to the shaven-headed pirate. Agona alone seemed beyond the power of fear or the unexpected. He rose slowly, taking the cat into his arms, where the poor creature nestled as if for its last hope of protection.

This, for a moment only, struck Chris as curious, for it was Agona who had made the astounding transformation of the boy into the cat. And yet there was so little that was fearful about the horned Negro, giant though he was, that with the next second Chris had dismissed the strangeness from his mind. For if Agona had transformed the boy for his own safety against the evil of Mamba — for fearsome *she* most certainly was — then it would only be Agona who could, if this was possible, bring the child back to himself and his own form. The coughing gusts of the pirate's rasping laughter made Chris's attention swing back to the audience of two.

The pirate and his hunchbacked henchman were a study in opposing expressions. Claggett Chew's set mask of selfish brutality seemed to find painful the laughter he permitted himself so grudgingly and so seldom but now could not resist, while the miser Simon Gosler's thin lined face was as aghast as it is possible for a human face to be. Just as Chris's notice reached the two men, Chew rolling from side to side in his chair and slapping his thighs, Simon Gosler thrust his dirty-nailed hands into his hair in a gesture of total despair.

"Where is a nation's ransom money now?" his nasal voice rose to a screech. "What have you now but a cat? Fools! Fools!"

Yet although he said "fools," his look and his voice were directed solely at Claggett Chew. This boisterous individual began to slow his long-drawn-out explosions of mirth, wiping his eyes with both hands. It was one of the few occasions when Chris was ever to see the whip laid aside, for it seldom left Claggett Chew's heavy white hand.

"Well done!" shouted Chew at last to Agona. "I never saw a better trick in my life! Here!" and he tossed a heavy leather bag that clinked in the direction of Agona. It fell at the big Negro's feet; he made no move to recover it, but with a mur-

mur indicated to one of the slaves to pick up the sack from the crushed snow.

Mamba, glaring at the heavy bag of gold or silver pieces, darted looks at Agona that were no less venomous than had been those of the copperhead snake whose body still lay at her feet, wrenched by the spasms of its long dying. That she had failed to make a soulless zombie of Jean-Jacques, to be one of the band of seemingly dead men and women surrounding Claggett Chew who did what they were told, unable to act or think or move of their own free will; that she had had struck out of her hands before the slaves and her master the instruments of her ritual, left Mamba in a crestfallen silent rage. Her eyes were more than ever somber with the ugliness of her thoughts as she stared, muttering, at Agona and the cat. Her brief vigor during the power of the ritual dance and the incantation of the snake had vanished like the tearing away of a veil, and she

145

was left what she was, an old woman of too many years for counting, and a dangerous enemy.

What a crew! thought Chris, Simon Gosler rocking now as Claggett Chew had been but a little before, but not for the same reasons. Gosler, miser that he was, rocked from frustration and hopelessness. His well-laid plan, his prize of gold and his human prize almost beyond price, had been transformed — by what African magic he did not know — into a cat, no longer the son of a king and a king himself.

"A cat!" he wailed, clutching handfuls of his filthy lank hair. "Who will *believe* that a boy stood there? Who wants a cat? They are two-a-penny, good only for mousers or drowning! Ai-yai! Ai-yai-yai!"

With the speed with which he was capable, Claggett Chew suddenly stiffened in his chair, and grasping its arms, slowly rose, rigid with suspicion.

"There is a spy about — I feel it — I know it!" he growled.

Chris inwardly shuddered and cast from his mind all thoughts but those that held him in his disguise. For a moment he wondered if he should change to some other form, but decided that any smallest motion would attract Claggett Chew's sensitive attention. So he remained as, and where, he was. But he shook in himself, for he had knowledge from the past of the extent of Chew's magicianship.

For a few minutes Claggett Chew stood swaying, the tall bulk of him made larger by the fur-lined cape sweeping from his shoulders to the ground. He swayed as a dog will, testing the air as it searches for a scent, and Chris imagined that he could almost feel the power of the pirate's ability, sifting the atmosphere in search of an invading watcher.

146

With an abrupt shrug, Chew threw his cape off, leaped into
the ring of fires, and with a wide swing of his arms, sent the
slaves, Mamba, Baka and Agona, running into the open door
of the shed. At a second command, this time a guttural
shout, the blind-eyed zombies, men and women, rose like sleep-
walkers and shuffled after them, off the trampled snowy
ground, while the humpback limped hurriedly into the wing,
muttering and moaning to himself, and slamming the door to
behind him. Claggett Chew was left alone in a ghastly quiet.

The essence of winter seemed held in that bleak square, and
Chris, high on the willow tree, felt alone as he never had before.
Claggett Chew strode into the center of the space, the thirteen
fires smoldering red around him, and began slowly to turn,
looking, it seemed, at every tiniest thing as he moved.

Not stirring from where he stood, he turned slowly, slowly.
Now the long wing with its hastily slammed door lay before

him, and still he turned, the whip hanging like a live thing from his hand. All Chris's thoughts and forces were fixed on holding to the twig and with keeping his leaf shape, as still Claggett Chew continued to turn.

Chew's eyes passed the main part of the house, and now swept along the near wing. Chris shivered, and as he did so, the deep-set eyes came to the willow tree. The pirate's glance crept up the trunk of the tree, still partly dressed in a few tattered yellow leaves and crusts of snow. With the force of lightning came the inevitable shout of triumph.

"Aha! A maple leaf — upon a willow tree! A green, green leaf upon a sallow tree!"

The man's face, his teeth grinding in his victorious power, was frightful to contemplate.

"I have you now, you little spy! *This* time I have you! You shall not escape Claggett Chew!"

The whip spun up above his head. Around and around, as he stood straddle-legged in the center of the circle of fiery embers, whirled the sinuous, pliable whip. Fast and faster it wheeled above his head, whistling through the air, and as it spun, the wind began softly to rise. From out of the breathless night came a first whisper of air. Then a sigh touched the smallest of the twigs, the most delicate of the grasses. Circling still, round and round went the whip high over Claggett Chew's head. The fires threw a rising sinister red glow up his booted legs, to be echoed in his deep-set eyes, giving them a false warmth.

Over the roofs of the house and far distant, from the very peak of the sky, Chris could sense a ferment in the air, a seething unrest spinning first one way and then another, as if re-

148

sisting an imperious and feared summons. The wind whimpered along the banks of the stream like a whipped dog. It crept forward from far down at the end of the pasture. The willows marking the line of the running water began to bend; the tops of the trees all about, to curtsy and to bow.

Chris felt the growing tug of the air about him and knew what to expect. He was as determined to hold on as Claggett Chew was to dislodge him, and yet he wondered if a change to some other shape would be possible or feasible.

As if in reply to his thought a blast of wind roared out of the sky to shake the windows of the house, send the branches of the trees clashing against one another, and blow a heavy spray off the waterfall against the end of the building and the stone chimney. All vestige of snow was now gone from the trees, blown off entirely, and Chris, taken by surprise, even though he had thought to anticipate such a move, had time to do nothing more than hold on for his life.

And still the wind rose. At Riveridge the shutters on the windows of the guest wing tore loose and banged, as if to rouse any sleepers there still might be. Old Mrs. Moffit lifted her head in its nightcap from her pillow and rang for Selena to go about the house to see that all was well. When the sleepy shivering girl had returned, the wind still blowing harder, the old woman was sitting up in bed, a shawl over her shoulders.

"This is most untoward," she said. "This wind bodes no good, for it smacks of a hurricane. Run, Selena, and look out from the upper hall window. See if Jonah and Uncle Borb are about in the quarters, for I hear distant shutters rattling. Someone must go over to the guest wing. And see to the fires, Selena, too, that no spark be blown out from the fireplaces to set

150

us all alight." And as Selena moved to do her bidding, the old lady put out her hand to detain her once more. "Stay! Bring me another candle and my spectacles. There. I shall read a little from the Bible, for I like not this wind. It is like no equinoctial gale I ever knew. Hark! A brick was blown clean off the chimney! What did I just say!" and settling her spectacles more firmly on her nose and pulling her shawl more closely about her, Mrs. Moffit opened the Bible and began to read, lifting her head to listen from time to time.

It was a gale spoken of for generations after, for there was never another like it in that part of the world within men's knowledge. As for Chris, he held on against the tearing, blistering force of the howling air that seemed to claw at his vitals, pounding from all sides at his thoughts and his strength. He held on for several harrowing, freezing hours, forcing his waning vitality, and in his mind, gritting his teeth to hold — hold — hold.

But he was up against a force and a man stronger, that night, than he was, and as the wind rose and rose, screaming and sobbing as the whip circled inexorably above the head of Claggett Chew, the wind finally succeeded. The branch on which was a twig held to by a green maple leaf was broken from the willow trunk. Thrown to the ground in a jumble of noise, snapping branches, and furious storm, Chris, exhausted and shocked by the fall, relaxed for a second.

That second was too long. He remembered later the sneering exultation on his enemy's white face. Then he was whirled into a blackness of fatigue in which he knew nothing.

CHAPTER 19

HRIS CAME TO HIM-self with a sickening twirl-ing motion. At first, his brain and senses spinning, he thought he was still falling, the branches cracking from under him and the earth rushing up to meet him. Instead, as his mind cleared, he found to his amazement that he was still in his leaf-shape and was being twirled between the finger and thumb of no less a person than Claggett Chew himself.

With an inner gasp of horror, he held on to his reeling thoughts long enough to realize that he was in a room comfort-ably furnished, and before a blazing fire. Claggett Chew, sit-ting at his ease near a branched candlestick, was whirling the maple leaf between his fingers and muttering to himself.

"Clever! Clever! No denying — it is a shrewd disguise. But it is your last, you little sneak! For I shall singe you lightly and slowly all around. The candle will do for a start — and the fire be a fine warm finish. For I am tired of being confounded by a lad of tricks!"

There was not a second to lose. Chris, spun though he was,

152

first one way and then the other, gathered together the remnants of his strength, realizing that a carpet with a design on it covered the floor. Seizing upon the smallest section of the design that he could clearly follow, with all his will the boy repeated the incantation of the change within himself even as the pirate held out the leaf toward the candle flame.

For Chris there was the soft interior jolt of the change; for Claggett Chew there was nothing left between his outstretched fingers except empty air and a diminishing feeling of satisfaction. So close had he held the leaf that the evil man actually burned his own fingers, staring in stupefaction for a long moment at his hand. Then the low-ceilinged room resounded with oaths, loud and violent, as Chew, springing up from his chair, began looking everywhere for his prisoner.

"By my blood and bones!" he ground out from between his clamped teeth, "you are still here, that I am sure of!" he cried. "Hide where you will, Claggett Chew shall find you! By the gizzard of a toad — I shall get you yet, nimble though you may be!"

So saying, the heavy man stamped about the room while Chris, a part of the border design of the rug, wished he had the time and safety to change into a fly — a mouse — anything else, to be far from the crushing weight of the pirate's shifting boots.

Claggett Chew was examining the ceiling minutely. Next the furniture and every corner, pulling back the curtain that covered a window to the west, overlooking the courtyard and the waterfall. To Chris's unspeakable relief he did not seem to think of looking at the carpet. Robbed of his prey, he was so infuriated by his own rage and frustration that he was no

153

longer entirely master of himself.

At last he gave up the search for the time being. Standing in the center of the room he glared about him, his head bent forward to miss the low ceiling that he otherwise might have scraped with his shaved bristly skull.

"You are here!" he shouted. "I know it! And you are human — you will hunger and you will thirst! I shall leave you here — you cannot escape — and in good time you will be in your own shape and on your knees, begging Chew for bread and water! So — until that time — fast well, and good appetite!" and the pirate strode from the room, his whip in his hand. Slamming the door, Chris heard the key turn in the lock with a *clack!* followed by the sound of Claggett Chew's feet clattering down the stairs that were evidently just outside.

For perhaps an hour Chris held to his cramped and uncomfortable shape as a small portion of the design in the worn carpet. Then, hearing Claggett Chew shouting orders outside, to the slaves or the inarticulate zombies, Chris dared return to himself.

The relief was enormous. It had been many hours since he had been his usual self, and Chris stretched deliciously in every direction. This refreshed him briefly, but he understood the cunning behind his captor's simple plan, for, being a healthy boy of fourteen, Chris was already ravenously hungry, and thirsty into the bargain.

He made a quick tour of the room. This, Claggett Chew's bedchamber, ran along the length of the main part of the house, from back to front, with a stone fireplace in the center wall, to the left, and a window at either end. Going to the first window near the only door and peeping out, Chris saw that the

morning was far advanced on a gray raw day. No one was to
be seen in the square below, where the voodoo ritual had taken
place the night before, so Chris took courage enough to tiptoe
across the uneven floor to peer out from the other side.

The second window, looking east, was a little to the left, and
above the front door. Chris remembered having seen Claggett
Chew and Simon Gosler rush out through it with lanterns, the
night he and Mr. Wicker had watched from the hill across the
road. Chris gathered, with a quickening pulse, that the second
window, at which he had seen the boy Jean-Jacques, must be to

his left in the wing, and that they shared the same chimney.

Below him he could see Claggett Chew, a wool muffler about his neck and his whip in his hand, directing the packing of bolts of cloth into a cart. The bolts were covered with sacking but their colors showed through rents here and there. The dyeing vats must be, Chris pondered, on the ground floor of the wing next door.

Claggett Chew seemed well occupied, at any rate for a short while, and Chris lost no time in seeking a way out of his prison. Changing himself into a mouse he ran along the skirting board of the room, pressing his mouse-nose under the door as far as it would go. He made an investigation of the whole room, trying the possibilities of every crack, but not one was large enough to let a mouse through.

Undefeated, Chris took the shape of a fly — one of his favorite changes. The fly buzzed busily over to one window, crawling around it inch by inch. Not even space for a fly to soar to freedom. The second sealed window was no better. Again, he tried to creep under the door where, as a mouse, he had failed, but there he was met with Claggett Chew's magic, for although there was space enough for a fly to pass, he came up against an invisible barrier, as of a strong wind. It blew steadily under the door with greater force than a fly could muster, try as he did for several hours, to fly or creep past, against it.

Discouraged and worn out, hungry and thirsty, Chris, after listening carefully to be sure that his enemy was out of the way, retook his own shape to rest himself and leaned disconsolately on the side of the hearth, looking with dispirited eyes at the dying fire.

The afternoon was melting into frosty night. Chris stared,

156

tired to his bones, at the embers, and as he stared, he began to notice the back of the fireplace.

While the border of the hearth was, like the chimney, of fieldstone, the back of the fireplace appeared to be of metal, embossed with a coat of arms that was blackened and undecipherable from soot and smoke. In the sudden grip of a wild hope, Chris, burning his hands on the hot metal, reached over the low embers that were all that was left of the earlier blaze of logs. With a pulse of excitement in his throat that threatened to suffocate him, he pressed and pounded on the fireback. His hands black and his coat sleeves singed, he was ready to give up when he thought he heard a faint sound. Holding his breath to listen he heard it again: it was the definite *miaow* of a cat. Chris, his heart leaping, began once more to press and pound — not so hard as to arouse Chew's suspicions, however — going over every inch of the fireback.

With a lurch and a scrape, the fireback began to move. Slowly, with a barely perceptible creak, it slid back into a niche in the wall.

Chris, breathless, looked through, across a second smoldering fire, to see a yellow cat standing on its hind legs, pressing on the fireback from its side, with its forepaws. Just at that moment, with a cold stab of fear, Chris heard from the bottom of the stairs Claggett's voice saying, "I shall see how the prisoner fares, Simon, and eat my dinner and drink my wine before him, to give him a good appetite."

With a scurry, bending double and feeling the heat through the soles of his shoes, Chris scrambled through into the room beyond, and, directed by the paws of the cat and by the eloquence of its enormous eyes, he pressed on the spot it indicated. Even as the fireback began to slide slowly, reluctantly back, the clump of Claggett Chew's boots could be heard outside the bedroom door.

CHAPTER 20

*T*OGETHER, FOR A hushed second, cat and boy held their breath. But the weighty iron fireback slid silently across between the two rooms before two pairs of eyes, fearfully staring at the final diminishing crack, could see more than the opening of the bedroom door. Both guessed what would follow. Roars of rage instantly ripped the air in the room beyond. Chris, with a long letting-out of breath, turned to look at the animal beside him.

Many as were the weird things that Chris had seen in this other world of the past, the yellow cat was perhaps the most eerie, because it was so nearly natural. Its overlarge head and hunched body were catlike enough; it was the eyes that gave Chris's heart a dread turning-over of horror. For in that cat-mask of yellow fur, below the pointed ears, were set two eyes that were not those of a cat at all. They were human eyes; the eyes of a frightened lonely boy.

Looking for a moment deep into the eyes that met his with such agonized meaning, unmindful of the oaths seeping through

the wall of Claggett Chew's room, Chris's own eyes filled with tears he could not check, and his horror mounted as he saw tears well up in the cat's eyes in answer to his own and roll one by one down the orange furry face. With a spontaneous gesture of protection and sorrow, Chris put out his arms. His face, too, must have shown his understanding of who and what confronted him, for the cat rushed into the proffered arms to put its head, with a most unfeline gesture, on Chris's shoulder. Chris was on the point of giving way to the grief and fright that filled his own heart to overflowing, but Claggett Chew's temper seeming to rise, he gulped back the lump of pity gathering in his throat for the transformed boy in his arms, and perhaps a little for himself, at the desperate circumstances by which he was hemmed.

The danger of the situation occupied by Jean-Jacques and himself brought him back to the instant need for action. If the house had been built by Simon Gosler, as he guessed, Claggett Chew might not know of the sliding panel at the back of the fire. But Chew even at that moment might be searching for the place to press to release the spring, and Chris was still in his own form.

Looking frantically around the room he had just entered, he found it to be a bedroom too, but only a makeshift one. There was, as in Claggett Chew's room, a window at either end, a simple bed, a chair, but no wall. Chris tiptoed to the curtain hung across the length of the chamber. Putting his eye to a tear in the folds, Chris, even in the darkening light but little added to by the fire behind him, was taken aback.

For in front of him stretched the length of Claggett Chew's drying shed for his dyed stuffs. Blue, green, buff, plum; in lines and blocks of color they hung from wall to wall. Yard upon yard of drying materials made a series of curtains hung at about Chris's height from end to end of the forty-foot building. The colors swam together until the far end of the wing dissolved into the shadow of dusk and distance. The warmth of the curtained space that had been a prison for the French boy was caused, Chris reasoned, by a larger fireplace below, where the kettles of dye swung over the fire.

Whipping about he knelt, holding out his hands to the cat, who ran to him. Putting his hands on the cat's shoulders and looking intently at it, Chris began to whisper, watching in the gathering twilight to see if understanding lay in those human eyes, fixed on his.

"Can you understand me?"

The relief that washed over the terrified eyes before him was heart-rending to see.

"Nod your head if you do, Jean-Jacques!" Chris ordered, and with tears again running from its eyes at the sound of its

161

name, the poor cat nodded its head.

"Listen!" Chris whispered, at the cat's very ear. "There is no time to lose. At any minute Chew may come in, one way or another. I can change my shape, but he has magic powers too. I shall change myself into a mouse; you must hold me by the fur of my back, and play with me as real cats do. It is my only hope! I shall pretend to be dying. Please help!"

The eyes near his seemed to comprehend, but, hearing with a pang the yell of triumph as Claggett Chew found the spring of the panel, and the panel began to move, Chris said in a frenzy, "Nod if you understand!"

The cat nodded. In another instant a limp mouse hung in its jaws as it sat, placid, before the fire and looked straight into the evil face of the searching pirate. Claggett Chew, leaning across his own sulky fire, thrust his face above the smoke and looked to right and left.

"Where did he get to? Eh? Confound it — this is too small a space for me to pass! Ha! You are a mouser already? Good — good — yet, stay! That mouse — "

He appeared to be on the point of reaching out, but the cat, as if impatient, rose, carrying the mouse without haste well beyond reach. Tossing its burden into the air, the yellow beast put out a paw to pat at the poor creature as it tried to drag itself away. Claggett Chew burst into a shout of laughter, coughing in the smoke of the fire, his eyes watering, but evidently well pleased.

"Aye! That is a mouse that is no mouse! So — eat it up — let me hear you crunch its bones! I had an end well chosen for it; you provide me with another even better. Come — let me hear your teeth in its neck, or I shall come in and pinch its life

162

out between my fingers, and *that* it would please me well to do!"

The cat turned its back to the pirate, who began to fret at the hot bricks across which he supported himself and at the pungent wood smoke that teased his lungs and eyes. Glancing in hasty terror about it, the cat saw a chicken bone fallen under the bed from some earlier day when it had been a more privileged prisoner. Humping itself so that its head could not be seen and blotting out the mouse's body with its own, with a flip of its paw the cat had the bone in its mouth. Turning its head to one side, as cats do when they bite down on something, it cracked the bone with a clear sharp sound.

"Ah-ha! So — it is ended!" rumbled Claggett Chew. "Here — out of the way, that I may see that you do not dissemble!" and snatching the hearth brush, Chew made a sweep to brush away the cat and disclose the remains of the mouse.

The cat refused to be dislodged. Turning its head from side to side, it cracked the chicken bone for all it was worth. Meanwhile, in those precious seconds the hidden mouse, very much alive and aware of its danger, became a fly, which crept stealthily deep into the fur of the cat's neck.

No sooner was this done that the cat rose, lazily, licking its chops. It stretched first fore, and then aft; made itself into a cozy ball with its tail tucked neatly all around, and closed its eyes as it began to purr.

Claggett Chew, the broom suspended in mid-air, lowered it by degrees, ruminating the while. At last, his eyes going from the floor where the cat had been to the dozing animal purring with contentment, he let the hearth brush fall and stroked his ugly chin thoughtfully.

"Hm-mm," came from Claggett Chew. "It *appears* to be well taken care of, that mouse. Hm-mm. Who would have thought that such an easy way out for it would present itself? Well, well. Devil take those cinders! They are hot as the seven hinges!" He began to draw back into his own quarters but as he did so, touched his head with a wave of the hand in salute. "Thank you, boy — cat! Hunger does not pick and choose! You have served me well this day — better than you have catly knowledge of! I shall sleep well this night."

So saying, the evil man, cursing at the heat of the embers and

164

his scorched clothes, drew back into his own room and a moment later, sent the metal fireback gliding across.

Only then did the yellow cat spring up, trembling throughout its body, and racing in and out of the colored cloths, whitely scarred with the moonlight now coming through the several windows of the wing, ran to the farthest corner of the attic. There it huddled, shaking, until it fell into an uneasy sleep. And the moon was high, the cat in a profound slumber, before the fly again became a boy. Going silently to the nearest window, Chris looked out to see if anyone was about. But what he saw in the white frosty light woke him up more surely than if a bugle had sounded at his ear. He started, leaning forward with his face pressed against the glass, and his excited breath clouded the small square panes.

CHAPTER 21

HE STRONG WHITE light of a bright moon on hoarfrost drenched the empty square below where Chris stood. Standing at the end window of the long wing he had an excellent view of the waterfall behind the house. He could not see without a shudder the willow tree overhanging it, for the broken branch to which he had clung twenty-four hours earlier still lay on the bank near the top of the dam. What now held Chris's eyes was the somber figure under the willow tree.

It needed only a minute to discover the figure as that of Agona. The Negro's huge size instantly gave him away to any onlooker. The man, with powerful arms, was hoisting himself into the willow tree.

Chris watched, fascinated, as Agona swung himself hand over hand along the strongest branch of the tree that grew out over the width of the stream. The glassy water of the dam raced under him; soon he could swing himself to the farther bank. Ice crystals rimmed the grasses along even such swiftly running water, but Agona only hesitated long enough to lift his head to look about him. Chris hastily drew back, flattening himself close to the wall, and when a moment later he dared to peer out again, to his amazement he saw the giant pull off his shirt and his sisal shoes. Reaching down into the water under the bank, exactly where the shadow of the willow branch fell upon the water, the man with the leopard's teeth woven into his hair pulled out a length of stout rope. He held the rope end in his powerful hands; Chris, looking on in the silence broken only by the falling water, saw the giant twist the rope about his wrists and brace his bare feet into the bank. Sharply black and gray under the cold moon, the muscles under his skin began to bulge and move.

For several minutes the tall Negro strained. Gradually, as if pulling back on a heavy weight or force, something changed on the smooth surface of the water and Agona stepped back, slowly pulling.

Chris's attention was fixed on the water. It shone with an almost oily gleam as it gathered its strength at the barrier of the dam. On this sleek surface a cup-sized black hole appeared, which grew and spread. Then, with a slow sighing, sucking sound, the whole power of the stream rushed down a hidden cavity! The dripping weedy stone face of the dam gradually bared itself as Dragon Run poured away underground.

Flabbergasted, Chris's eyes were starting from his head, but he had no time to do more than watch, for he saw, coming silently from the door of the shed, on the left now from where he stood, the two slaves who had helped Agona in the ritual of the night before. Quite soundlessly they moved to the top of the dam, where, at a gesture from Agona, one after the other

167

poised and plunged into the swirling black hole where the water poured. Last, Agona himself, pointing like a dark arrow, flashed from sight.

For long Chris looked and waited. It was several hours later when Agona reappeared from the front of the house, running lightly. He loosened the rope from where he had secured it. The stream seemed of its own weight to force back the trap hidden in the stream bed, for it regained its usual appearance;

the dam refilled and poured over its stony wall once more. Agona hid the rope under the water in some crevice in the bank and disappeared into the shadows. Silence and white frost seemed to Chris so innocent that he found it hard to believe his eyes had not played him tricks. He shook himself and rubbed his face with his hands, forgetting that they were still black with soot.

No — he was awake, and as he looked up a familiar bird was

planing and drifting outside the window. Chris recognized it at once. It was Mr. Wicker come to discover what had happened to him.

As if by magic — which it could have been — the window near him opened. The boy needed no second invitation. Glancing at the cat and seeing that it still slept, he looked questioningly at the bird. He would dearly have loved to have taken the cat with him, but the bird wagged its head; the moment of rescue was not yet.

Out into the chill air rose a second bird. The roofs of the house and the wing, the icicles along the stream, dwindled as side by side the two birds flew high into the air. It needed all Chris's weakened strength to carry him back to Riveridge.

CHAPTER 22

*I*T WAS DURING Chris's profound sleep in Riveridge's guest wing, after one of Aunt Abby's delicious meals, that the monster reappeared. Not only outside the windows of the house; but there were marks of the panther pads in the slave quarters also. Selena, dozing outside the door of Mrs. Moffit's bedroom, had seen the fearsome head at the hall window; her screams of fright had roused other servants, who, running from their cabins, had been struck dumb with terror at the sight of the panther prints all around their doors.

Work was at a standstill all the next day, for not one of Mrs. Moffit's workers would venture out past the trail of the panther. Had not another light snow fallen to blot them from sight there is no telling how long fear would have held them indoors. Mr. Wicker, examining the marks in the daylight, looked thoughtfully at the large spaces between each print step. Six or eight feet was the least.

"What does it tell you, sir?" Chris asked, looking up at the studious face pondering, the slender fingers measuring. Mr.

Wicker at last stood, from where he had been kneeling in the snow, chafing his hands in the nipping air. Circling them, the small cabin windows were puckered with the faces of the fearful slaves, their eyes swollen with fright, not so much at what they had seen printed near their doors and on their pathways, but at a presence their eyes had not seen and that they trembled to guess at.

Mr. Wicker's voice was low; too low to carry beyond Chris.

"It tells me that the monster is a man, Christopher."

172

"A *man?*" Chris's eyes grew larger. "But sir — the panther-prints — "

Mr. Wicker nodded. "I know. Nevertheless, there is no such thing as a two-legged panther. It has to be a man."

Chris glanced around, thoughtful in his turn. "Claggett Chew, sir?" he asked.

Mr. Wicker turned to go back into the house, his hands under his coattails. His face was remote.

"Possibly, Christopher, but I do not think so. Whoever it is, is looking for something — or someone."

On the doorstep before the white door with its polished brass knocker, Chris's face suddenly lighted up.

"Agona, sir?"

"Who, my boy?"

Chris fairly danced in his impatience. "There hasn't been time to tell you, sir! This print business happened so fast and made such a fuss! Let me tell you all about it — er — " he laughed at himself and at Mr. Wicker's quizzical expression, " — that is, whatever you may not know already."

Sitting close over the sitting-room fire, this time with the curtains drawn, Chris told his master everything as it had occurred. Mr. Wicker listened with his usual impassive face, in which Chris could not read what the magician knew, or what small detail might have escaped him. When Chris had quite finished, Mr. Wicker, his long legs toward the fire and his fingertips together in his familiar relaxed and yet attentive position, nodded calmly.

"Yes, my boy. Just so. Claggett Chew *may* think you are inside the belly of the yellow cat and a nag to him no longer, and then again, he may not. I should not trust it, if I were

173

you. I rather fancy he must have had more wine than was good for him before he came upstairs, and that his wits were muddled, otherwise the chicken bone would not have taken him in so completely. Still," the magician said, sitting up in his chair, "let us hope for the best and be grateful for small mercies. For the time being, you are reasonably safe."

"Please, sir," Chris began, "I want to go back. That little boy — all alone. It isn't right to leave him — he's so frightened."

The neat chestnut head nodded as Mr. Wicker replied. "As indeed, who would not be? Well, young man, it may be wise for you to return, but until Agona turns the cat back into the boy he really is, it is folly to bring Jean-Jacques here." He paused, staring at the fire. "The person who needs to be guarded," said Mr. Wicker, "is Agona."

"*Agona?*" Chris was incredulous. "Why — he's a giant — twice as tall as I am, or very nearly. And strong! Who would harm him? Who *could* harm him, sir?"

Mr. Wicker smiled his dry, ironic smile. "You have forgotten old Mamba, my boy. Her cult is that of hate and evil. All that is now turned against Agona, who defied and routed her, and shamed her before her equals and her masters."

The magician's fine face was grave and Chris felt a weight of dread sinking like a plumb line to his very shoes.

"Yes, my boy. You had indeed better return, to keep your eye on Mamba. Remember! If aught befalls Agona, the cat remains a cat; the boy within is doomed. And then of course," he said with another somber smile, "there is always the little matter of Claggett Chew!"

Poor Chris felt as if he had a piece of lead for a heart, and lead soles to his boots. He looked across the hearth to his master's steady eyes, as if the quiet man facing him doubted that he would go, or could do any good, once there. Mr. Wicker's expression fired Chris and made him angry. He jumped up impetuously.

"I may not be a help, but I intend to go, sir! That boy might be me — in a body I couldn't get out of! I know just how it would feel. He has to have help — comfort — *something!* He's only about eight, sir!"

Mr. Wicker's expression did not change, he merely continued to look at Chris.

"I know, Christopher."

"So I'm going back, sir, *now*. In a minute. I wanted to ask you something first — "

"Ask away, my boy," said the magician, not moving. Chris paced nervously about the room, and finally came back to sit on the edge of his chair across from the relaxed, patient man.

"Sir — those zombies. Please tell me about them. I don't understand."

Mr. Wicker, intent at once, leaned forward. "No one quite knows about zombies. Except, perhaps, the African priests and priestesses of the Vodun, or Voodoo cult, Christopher. Some say that they are dead bodies, dug up, and by magic powers made to do the bidding of the Voodoo believers. These resurrected ones have no recollection of who they are, no memory of their past. They no longer have a will of their own; this is how they are forced to do whatever they are told without being able to refuse. They are dead-alives; seemingly hypnotized. They move as if in a trance."

Chris nodded reminiscently. "They do, sir — they did." A

175

silence fell and then he asked, "Is there no hope for these poor people? Must they go on forever, neither alive nor dead?"

The young face was troubled and earnest. Mr. Wicker looked back with compassion.

"Yes, Christopher, there is hope. Literally, a *grain* of hope. For should a grain of salt pass the lips of a zombie, then its memory returns. It will rush back to its grave, and never more be able to be raised from it. It is then dead beyond all possibility of resuscitation."

Chris's face cleared. "Good. Then something can be done for them, too."

Mr. Wicker's face was shadowed by a moment of anxiety. "Have a care, Christopher! Agona is perfectly aware of this fact. Yet you have seen him and the slaves who are loyal to him, and who are the keepers of the zombies, vanishing into the interior of the earth. Agona is a power for good — do not attempt to thwart him too soon, or you may turn good into evil. Even good must be done at its own speed." He smiled. "In its own good time."

Chris thought this over and then inquired, "What is the *kingolo* root that Mamba spoke of, sir? The liquid she held out to the boy?"

Mr. Wicker took his time in replying. At last he said, "*Kingolo may* be what causes zombies to behave as they do, my boy. It is rare — an ugly plant I am told, though I have never seen it myself. With glossy leaves and long lashlike stems springing from a common root. These whiplike tendrils burrow into the ground and so multiply on themselves. The root is a bright orange-yellow." Mr. Wicker sighed and shook his head. "It sounds an evil-looking plant."

176

"Then some sort of broth or brew is made from the root or the bark, sir," Chris pursued, "and to drink it — well — what *does* happen to those who drink it? They don't exactly die, so Mamba said — "

"No, Christopher. They probably go into what is called 'suspended animation.' They seem dead, but can be partially resurrected. Ugh!" Mr. Wicker shivered. "What a hateful subject, and what tragic creatures are the poor zombies!"

Chris lifted his eyebrows with a hopeful look. "Salt, sir?"

Mr. Wicker's mouth was grim. "Salt!" he replied cryptically. "By the way, my boy," he went on, "a small bag of salt under your head — or Agona's — while sleeping will fend off any spell Mamba could put upon you. Remember that."

"Yes, sir. Oh — how does Mamba get *kingolo* root here, if it's an African plant?"

Mr. Wicker looked at the boy with a smile of pride. He enjoyed the young mind that was never satisfied with anything less than the truth, and was endlessly searching, like a hunting dog, to flush the hidden partridge, Truth, from cover.

"I have heard it said, Christopher," the magician answered, "that the Vodun priests brought over roots of the *kingolo* plant when they were taken as slaves from their own lands. In the reeking holds of the slave ships they guarded it with their lives, hidden under their clothes. And since the West Indian islands to which so many of the Africans were taken are similar in climate to parts of Africa, the plant throve and grew."

Chris frowned. "Haiti — is its climate tropical?"

"Definitely, my boy."

"Hm-mm. Thank you, sir," the boy said. Then he rose with determination on his face. "Now, sir, with your permission — "

Mr. Wicker rose too. "Certainly, my boy. By all means." And then, as Chris headed for the door, the magician turned the boy's shoulders gently in the direction of the window. "This time the bird is best, Christopher. It is not dark. Let me raise the sash. There. Look out for crows that could turn into hawks! And remember Mamba!"

"Yes sir. I'll do my best, but I may need help — "

Mr. Wicker smiled his crooked smile. "If not help, then a good meal, now and again, eh my boy? Godspeed to you!" called the magician.

The bird was already high over the trees. Mr. Wicker sighed and shut the window.

CHAPTER 23

*C*HRIS HAD TAKEN the form of an owl, for the silence of its wings and its ability to blend into the dusk. With strong wingbeats the owl soared. The moon was still bright and the vast panorama of the countryside tempted it to sweep high and far for a few moments.

A distant rattle and creak reached its keen ears. Inclining downward on a slant, the trees and fields, faded by winter and by moonlight far below, slid back past the bird. Chris followed the sound, which came from somewhere on the road, and in no time caught up with a wagon and a team of horses. A glance at the figure driving made his heart leap. No other man would venture out in winter without a hat in the icy air, and no other man had so bleak and pale a head.

Claggett Chew! Driving to Georgetown with a wagonload of dyed stuffs, leaving Simon Gosler in charge of the slaves and silent zombies!

Chris took instant care that no owl's shadow, racing ahead of it as it flew, could attract the pirate's attention. In a split

179

second the bird had wheeled about and dashed for the welcome
dark of the wood behind it. Waiting and listening, the faint
sound of Claggett Chew's voice, bellowing for the ferryman
on the banks of the Shenandoah at Vestal's Landing, came back,
fragmentary, on the chill air. In his owl's plumage, Chris dared
to fly along the ice-starred river, perching in an evergreen,
where he was well hidden. He wanted to make sure that his
enemy was really on the Georgetown road and safely out of
the way. When presently he had been entirely satisfied, seeing on the road beneath him the pirate's absorption in driving
the heavily laden wagon over the bad mountain road, the boy,

enjoying his night-bird shape swooped back, skimming the trees, to the low white house.

Here, too, he made a careful survey. It was well that he did, for gliding over the roof he made out a crouching figure digging in the streambank near the second waterfall. The figure was busy and absorbed, and had chosen a place some distance below the second, smaller waterfall, where the stream turned, and where the bank was so steep and high that anyone kneeling there was hidden from any part of the house or upstairs windows.

Tilting its way in and out of the branches of the trees overhanging Dragon Run, the owl, silent as a feather, alighted on a branch directly over the busy figure and opened its owl-eyes as far as they would go.

It was Mamba. Wrapped in shawls, with her old head turbaned against the cold, she was engrossed in digging the earth of the bank. The earth along the stream was largely the gray-white soil known as marl. It was this and nothing else that Mamba seemed impatient of having; she had a small pile of the oyster-colored earth heaped beside her, but winter in the ground had hardened even more firmly the substance made of finely crushed limestone. It had lain there, made of century after century of crushed shells, under some ancient sea aeons ago at the beginning of the world. It took Mamba long, old as she was, and resistant as the marl was at being detached from its bed, but at last she had as much as she needed.

With a skill that her African childhood must have taught her, the old woman hid all trace of where she had been digging, and then, taking up the marl, she began a bobbing dance, crooning to herself as she fashioned the earth in her hands. Bowing

181

to the moon, and after many curious gestures taking small handfuls of water where the moon lay brightest, she mixed it with the heavy clay she was forming. Chris's owl-eyes could at last see what the evil crone was making.

It was a puppet, and quite evidently intended to represent Agona. Soon Mamba drew from the pocket of her apron a tiny pair of horns that could have been those of a young goat, but when put on the head of the puppet enhanced the impression it was meant to give of the big Negro. Next, Mamba drew from under her shawl a ragged shirt — one of Agona's, no doubt — and with scissors, needle, and thread fashioned a small replica. In a short while she had also made a pair of trousers to put on the figurine.

So, bit by bit, the old priestess dressed the image, and when all was completed, including tufts of hair stuck to the head of the doll, laced with dog's teeth in semblance of the leopard-teeth in Agona's hair, the evildoer cackled aloud with pleasure. Propping the puppet against a stone on the bank, Mamba eyed the sky, where the moon was slowly setting. She began to hurry. Chris watched in his owl form, deep in the blackness cast by the trunk of the tree, set far above the silver, black, and gray of Dragon Run below. He now understood the making of the puppet and all that went with this strange scene. Strange, because for Mamba's spell to be successful all depended on its being completed before moon-set.

Under him on the shore Mamba, whining a low monotonous song of unknown words, sounding to Chris like the sleepy drone of jungle birds, unfamiliar and without pattern, began a slow stamping dance in front of the doll and facing the descending moon. Forward and back, bend and straighten, the old

182

woman moved with greater and greater vigor until she was whirling on the narrow verge of the stream itself, under the high bank beside the chattering water. Just as she drew out something from her pocket, holding it tightly in her hand over her head, the moon began to dip over the trees in its final disappearance for that night. With a cry that was neither human nor animal, Mamba struck down at the puppet.

Simultaneously with her shriek, triumphant and satisfied, rising to enshroud the bird in the tree, the moon sank out of sight. As if the world had been plunged into a sack, the glitter was instantly blotted from the stream; the heavy shadows that had seemed cut from black paper were wiped out in the general gloom. Chris congratulated himself on having chosen to be an owl, for without its night-eyes he would never have been able to penetrate the total dark.

As it was, peering down, he saw the chuckling, grinning priestess carefully pick up the doll that for her was now Agona and, carrying it with rare delicacy, hide it deep in the bank under the very tree where the owl sat. Presumably the roots of the tall sycamore had been undermined at one time by unusually high spring floods, leaving a hidden cavity under the bank. Still cackling low to herself, and scratching with her earth-stained fingers to erase every trace of her footprints from the shore, the small bent figure hurried away to the shed. In a moment, Chris, straining to hear, caught the faint chock of wood on wood as the door of the shed closed behind her.

Waiting patiently, after what he deemed a safe while, Chris flew down to the edge of the stream and regained his own shape. The sky was whitening for another day as the boy looked in vain into the miniature cavern where Mamba had

184

hidden her doll. Try as he would, it was too dark to see. Hesitantly, but with resolve, Chris held to a tree root and leaning forward put his hand into the black void.

His fingers touched something; it was the puppet. Lightly, the boy investigated, and on a sudden his fingers touched something sticking out from the belly of the doll. It was a heavy silver pin, and Chris pulled it out to look at it. Like a minute dagger, it had been thrust into the vitals of the marl figure.

It was as Chris was dropping the pin into the leather bag of magic odds and ends hanging about his neck, that he remembered having touched something else, in the blackness. About to change to a fly, to creep, somehow, into the upper floor of the wing to find the cat again, or into the shed to see what Mamba was doing, Chris paused to try to call back to his mind what the feeling of that touch had been.

His fingers had touched a hard, cold coil, looped at the feet of the puppet. Beads of perspiration started out on the boy's forehead and a mighty shudder that was not due to the cold convulsed him.

What his fingers had brushed had been the puppet's guardian, a hibernating copperhead snake.

C H A P T E R 2 4

*L*ATER THAT MORN–
ing, Agona, carrying a
steaming bowl of food,
came out of the slave shed.
From behind him, there floated the voices of the slaves, singing
of their lost freedom and of their lost land. As the giant's
strides took him farther away, the words followed him:

In the old days, we found our way.
Even over the burnt-dry grass
Of rolling prairies, where the thorn-trees grow,
Where giraffe-herds graze, and elephants stand
Like gray stone mountains that flap their ears;
Even by trails where the lion treads;
Yet did we know where our home lay.

In the night, we knew how to avoid
The rhinoceros, of mighty horn,
Or water-buffaloes, fiercest of all.
Along the ways known to the gazelles,
Where flickering zebras trot; always,

186

Always! We knew which way our home lay.

Where is it now — which way does it lie?
Over what seas did the slave ships sail?
Toward what sun, toward what moon?
Under what stars did our captors sail?
On what sad sea that we never saw?
Tell us, how shall we find our home?

Agona headed for the dyeing vat, going through the door that opened to the square, and up the stairs to the drying attic. Walking straight to the bedroom, the giant brushed aside the makeshift curtains and paused.

The curtained room was dusky, the low fire giving scarcely a glow. Crouched near it was the yellow cat, sleepless. Chris, a fly perched on Agona's shoulder, noticed that, unlike real cats, the eyes of this one did not glint green in the dark.

Agona began making crooning noises of comfort and invitation, and setting down the bowl near the cat, stroked its head and urged it to taste the food. After a moment the cat, ending a long questioning look into the dark kindly face above it, rose and began to eat, with many waits to glance about it fearfully, and to watch the face of Agona for any change of expression.

Agona smiled, a free happy smile of relief as the animal ate, and went forward to build up the fire into a good blaze. When the cat had eaten its fill, Agona took up the bowl and finished what remained in it for his own meal. The fire burning brightly and the sun beyond the windows growing stronger, so that the mists were slowly melting, the big black Negro took the cat on his knee and began to murmur to it in a low tone.

Chris, from where he was placed, could narrowly watch the expression in the cat's eyes, and it came to him all at once that the cat understood the — to Chris — unintelligible murmur. Chris cast about in his mind for what to do, for he felt every second to be of vital importance. He must know what was being said — but how?

The bag of magic odds and ends! But to get at that he must regain his own form! Well — dangerous it was, but it must be done.

Flying unseen and unheeded off Agona's shoulder, the fly flew over the curtain, and behind it, rapidly became himself and plunged his fingers into the mouth of the bag at his neck.

His fingers touched a small round object. Chris drew it out. It looked a little like a pebble, and for a moment the boy held it in his hand, puzzling over what it was to be used for. Abruptly he knew, for he had seen, in the ears of deaf people, something like it. Their stone was connected with an electric wire that helped their hearing. Perhaps this —

Chris put the magic stone into his ear. Sure enough, a magic hearing aid it was, for not only could he hear Agona's murmur but the words were now understandable.

What a superb gadget for tourists in foreign countries! Chris thought to himself. Why, everyone could understand everyone else, and misunderstandings would be almost impossible. The United Nations should have this, for it translates the sounds as they come to my ear, without the need of a translator!

Agona's deep voice was saying: "So you see, it was the only way you could be saved. If you will have faith in Agona, he will hide you where neither Mamba nor Claggett Chew can touch or harm you. Then you shall take back your own shape.

188

But it needs the courage of waiting."

Chris was revolving a plan in his mind as he listened. It was bold, but Chris, so often in danger yet never used to it, had felt the unmistakable brush of electric current about him that meant that some new danger, like a terrible bird, was fanning the air with its approaching wings. On an impulse, Chris, in his own shape, took his courage and his heart in his hands and walked past the curtains to face the man with the yellow cat upon his knee.

Lightning-fast, Agona, surprised, was on his feet with a knife in his hand, a knife with a blade as thin and as deadly as the tongue of a dragon. The cat, its back arched in fright and its tail swollen with its surprise, stood on its toes on the hearth with its eyes larger than ever.

"Peace, Agona!" Chris said. "I am here to help you both — not to harm!"

The giant's face relaxed. The pointing finger of death that he held, disappeared once more into his belt, and a slow smile began to ease the startled face.

"Are you the cause of the Big Wind? The spy that made my master so angry?" he asked in his deep throaty voice. Chris smiled.

"I am that one. I am an old enemy of your master's; I am here to help this boy, for I know the change that you made."

Agona turned to look at the cat with concern in his face, and motioned to Chris to draw near the fire. Chris did so, sitting cross-legged with his back to the flames, his arm about Jean-Jacques, both looking up at Agona, who sat with his huge hands on his knees, a thoughtful expression in his eyes.

"I have something to tell you, Agona, and something to give you," Chris began. And reaching into the bag at his throat he pulled out the silver pin that Mamba had speared into the belly of the puppet. Chris held it out to Agona as he told what he had seen.

When he had ended his story, the big man muttered, "I had a strong pain just at that time. Here." He put his hand on his stomach. "And a little while after, the pain went." He nodded his head seriously. "Agona knew what the old woman was up to. She will try other things — " he said with conviction. He looked down at the upturned faces of the boy and the cat. "Let Agona take the cat to safety, to the protection of the Dragon, who is hidden well."

Chris looked dubiously at Agona, then at the cat, which turned its apricot-colored furry face to gaze at the boy with its human eyes.

"The Dragon?" Chris queried.

Agona nodded. "This stream all about is the Dragon's stream, and hides it well. There, beside the Dragon, the boy will be safe!"

"When would you take him — " Chris began when a raucous bellow thundered up the stairs from below.

"Agona! Devil take your hide! Are you working this day, or idling it away in sleep up there? Come down and build this fire — there is work to do!"

Simon Gosler's voice rattled up like a handful of gravel, thrown at their ears. Agona started up, laid a finger to his lips, and with long strides was on his way down the stairs.

"Just seeing were the new-dyed pieces dry, master!" he said as he went, and Simon Gosler relapsed into sulky mutterings. The warmth grew as the fire below sprang like a host of fiery warriors in burnished armor up the chimney to the liberation of the cold morning air.

Chris leaned his lips to the ear of the cat. "I dare not keep my own form," he whispered. "I shall see what I can see in some other." He waited to see if Jean-Jacques had understood him, and the cat nodded, wide-eyed. Chris leaned forward again.

"I think something is going to happen," he whispered. "To-night!"

The cat looked at him, nodding hard, its eyes terrified.

191

CHAPTER 25

*P*ERCHED ON THE chimney-top of the house in the guise of a chickadee, Chris looked down as Baka herded the male zombies to fields across the road, beyond Dragon Run, while the young Negress followed after, leading out the women zombies. The two lines of zombies looked like people in a dream, their faded cotton and calico clothes in dim shadow-colors. Not a single shawl or jacket for warmth was to be seen, for zombies feel neither heat nor cold. Both Baka, far ahead, and the young Negress carried broad-bladed machete knives. They tapped the blades with a piece of iron, and the rhythmic metallic beat seemed to bind a web of sound about the slaves. Before long the dry shuffling of their feet had faded from the air.

Chris, in the form of the tiny black-capped bird, preened his feathers and waited. From the larger wing came an indistinct mingling of voices, with an occasional bad-tempered shout from Simon Gosler. Flying down in an arc, as he passed a window of the wing Chris had a glimpse of the hunchback, nursing his peg leg as he sat on an upturned cask watching the slaves at work over the dyeing kettles, swearing at them in an effort to make them work faster.

As the sun rose higher into the green-tinged blue of the fall sky, the winter that had come too soon receded briefly and the trees shone with autumn color. The atmosphere of a patterned workday wrapped the hour. Chris thought that every day must seem so to the slaves, and — had they been capable of thought — to the zombies. Far off, through the bleakening trees, Chris could see the slow lines of the dead-alive slaves, appearing and reappearing over the roll of the land, Baka leading one line, the young girl the other. The skirts of the women rose up over the curve of the brick-colored Virginia soil like faded flowers, dead before their bloom, or of inanimate things — the grays of lichens, browns of fallen leaves or of dried ferns, stone-blues, and the bleached yellow of dry grass.

Chris was wondering what direction to take next when Mamba came cautiously out from the slaves' shed. Wrapped in shawls and gnashing her toothless gums, the venomous old hag sent a glance of hate in the direction of the wing, muttering meanwhile. Chris felt it likely that her look was equally divided between Agona and Simon Gosler. She stood still, listening for a moment. From the far side of the wing the stamp of horses could be heard. Chris was instantly pierced with the fear that Claggett Chew might have returned, and flew to the peak of the roof to look over. But it was a second team, perhaps to go to Charles Town later in the day for supplies.

Flying back to his first perch, Chris found that Mamba was making her way down the steep bank of the stream and was about to wade across below the first waterfall. Holding her

worn slippers in her hand and clutching her skirts with the
other, with many stifled cries at the icy touch of the water, the
old woman started slowly over. She waded where a sandbank
made a shallow footing.

The better to observe what she intended doing, Chris flew
over the stream to a shrub growing on the bank near the dam
and the waterfall. The green glossy leaves showed no touch
of frost; the thorns on the long stems of the plant made a good
perch for a small bird.

Though watching Mamba's slow progress intently, Chris

began to feel a drowsiness coming over him. He must be more tired than he had realized, he thought, for sleep was lying ever more heavily on his eyelids. He had no desire to move; a gentle dizzy spin began in his head. The L-shaped house swung from side to side before his eyes and then began to turn, revolving around and around in an indistinct haze. With a wrench of effort, Chris groggily came awake to his danger, and with all his force fluttered off the shrub to sink to the ground under a tuft of grass near the water's edge. In a few minutes the boy's brain cleared. He felt his will and ability returning to him and looked with haggard keenness at the shrub.

Long tendrils of the thorny plant were embedding themselves all around a common root, and the root itself, where
something had scraped away the outer bark, showed a sullen
orange.

The *kingolo* root! Mamba had planted it on her arrival in
this new land, and the deadly plant had flourished with the
tenacious strength of evil growths and weeds. A fume of
noxious essence must come, undetectable, from the *kingolo*,
and Chris took a deep breath of the fresh air where he now
found himself.

Mamba, meanwhile, was clambering up the bank. First she
looked closely at the ground at the base of the *kingolo* bush.
Chris, drawing back even farther under the protecting bend
of the grasses, could hear and see perfectly, only a few feet
from where the old priestess was mumbling.

"Knife buried in ground, blade down, three nights," she was
saying, "evil spirits from the ground go into blade with magic
power!"

She parted some weeds and Chris could just make out the
top of a handle which could have been that of a small knife.

Mamba covered over the handle with the weeds, sighing
broken African words and phrases. Moving more quickly, the
wrinkle-faced crone cut deep into the ground with a long-
bladed knife which she drew from under her apron. With a
twist of her hand she cut a piece of the poisonous plant-root
from underground. Another moment and she had thrust her
hand down and brought it from the earth holding a fragment
of the yellow root. Wrapping it in a ragged cloth embroidered
with symbols, the old woman hurried away. Not even she was

safe against the exhalations of the *kingolo* which respected no one, not even Mamba.

Scarcely had Chris seen her go into the shed and was preparing to follow her, when a commotion took place on the far side of the wing. The horses whinnied and tossed their heads so that their harness jingled, and voices overlapped in surprised exclamations. Flying over to the rooftop Chris stretched his chickadee's head forward to see what was happening.

A Negro boy lay face downward in a faint on the ground, just outside the door of the wing. Simon Gosler and the two slaves were standing uncertainly above the fallen figure. Chris, looking directly down, felt his head swim once more at the sight of the back of the boy.

The young boy's shirt hung in shreds from his shoulders and and his back was a series of lash cuts, raw and bleeding. As Chris peered over, one of the slaves threw a bucket of water on the boy's dark close-cropped head. The lad gave a shudder of returning consciousness and lifted himself slowly, his head hanging. Then, seeing the peg leg and the one good foot of Simon Gosler near him, he said, "Take me, master! I'm a runaway! Take me to work for you!" and as he spoke, turned up his face.

It was Amos.

CHAPTER 26

*MOS! WITH WHIP* cuts on his back that would remain throughout his life, to confess with their telltale stripes the criminal or the slave!

Chris's heart was full, and his head swam at the shock of seeing his friend's pain-creased face. Why, Amos is no slave — has never been one! Chris angrily argued in himself. What's this? He really is beaten — those cuts aren't make-believe.

As he looked and wondered, flying down to perch on a wagon wheel for a better view, out of the door came Agona. Amos, half fainting with pain, lifted his drooping head once more, and his eyes and the eyes of the towering man met in an understanding glance. Chris, looking on and searching both faces, felt that although the two had never met before, some private intelligence passed from Amos to Agona, and an immediate comfort was returned to the miserable boy from the man standing silently in the sunlit door, the black square of the dyeing room behind him.

Simon Gosler's eyes were shining with greed, for here was a slave at no cost. Runaway, yes; but Simon knew how to hide what he wished to keep, and any master who would come looking for a lost boy would be met with a bland commiserating stare and a negative shake of the head. The humpback turned nervously to Agona.

"Here, Agona — help the boy to the room upstairs. Something must be put on those cuts, or he will not be fit to work today."

Work! Today!

That was too much for Chris. While the attention of Gosler and the slaves was engaged in helping to support the groaning Amos, no one noticed a darting bird that flew straight into the workroom and up the stairway. By the time Agona's feet were heard on the stairs, moving up slowly at the pace of the almost fainting lad, Chris had resumed his own shape, thrust his fingers hopefully into the leather bag at his neck, and felt the smooth sides of a round box.

What a host of memories that box called forth when it lay in his palm! The whip cut — now only a white line — along his jaw, given him one morning on the Georgetown docks by Claggett Chew, had been healed at once with the salve it held! Chris's eyes shone as he saw it, for he knew its healing powers, magical in their speed and in the instant soothing of pain. So it was with an expression in which confidence and concern were blended that he stood waiting as Agona and Amos came slowly into the little curtained room. The yellow cat had been sitting on the sunny window sill and had evidently seen what had gone on below. It jumped down to the floor by way of welcome, its eyes sad for another hurt creature.

Tears were not far from the eyes of the two friends when they met under such distressing circumstances, but Amos's good face lighted with relief when he saw Chris awaiting him, and he straightened up, wincing at what the gesture did to his raw back.

"You all right, Chris?" were his first low words, and when his friend nodded, his eyes shining too brightly at the courage and affection he saw in Amos's resolute expression, Amos added, "Then it was worth it!"

Not understanding, Chris motioned to the bed. "Agona," he said softly, so that his voice should not carry down to Simon Gosler, "I have a special salve that will heal his cuts at once. This is Amos, my friend — and Amos, this is Agona, who is a friend, too. Lie face down on the bed, now, and let me put this salve on. Remember how it healed the cut Claggett Chew gave me, down on the docks?"

Amos managed a grin. "Certainly do, Chris! Now I *know* I'll be all right!"

Agona stood silently by as Chris gently applied the magic salve, flinching at the ugly raw welts more than Amos did. When his back had been treated, Amos sat up with a sigh of ease, turning a grinning happy face to the big quiet Negro, the cat, and Chris.

"Surely is remarkable stuff, Chris! My back feels good as it always does — did. Mm-mm! Jonah did a true job on my back, no denying — "

"*What?*" Chris gasped, with difficulty keeping his tone down. "You didn't say *Jonah?*"

Amos grinned more widely than ever with mischievous satisfaction. "Certainly did. Uncle Borb's son, Jonah. Good

200

friend of mine, is Jonah."

Chris shook his head as if he had made a deep dive and had water in his ears.

"I can't be hearing right, Amos," he persisted. "I can't believe it — Jonah wouldn't do a thing like that. You'll have to explain." He turned his head from where he sat on the edge of the bed to look up at Agona's intent, thoughtful face. "Jonah is such a nice boy. He's the son of the housekeeper at Riveridge — Aunt Abby's son — " he was saying, when at the mention of Aunt Abby's name Agona was shaken as by a bolt of lightning. He reached forward and his huge hand grasped Chris's shoulder so hard that Chris thought his bones would crack under the mighty fingers.

"*Abby*, you say?" the big man demanded. "*Abby?*" His eyes bored into Chris's astonished look as if he would ferret the answer from the very brain of the boy before him.

"Why, yes. Agona, you're hurting my shoulder. Yes, Aunt Abby has been with Mrs. Moffit for years. Since she was a child, I think. Why do you — "

"*Agona!*" came Simon Gosler's exasperated howl from the foot of the stairs. "I did not ask you to nurse him back to health! Leave him alone and get back to work. My blood and bones!" he snarled. "We shall never have a good morning's work done with all these interruptions! *Agona!* Get down those stairs!"

Agona, a strange look of tenderness on his face, almost of happiness, turned without further word and went down to resume his work. Chris thought over the giant's behavior and question for a moment, but, finding no immediate answer and being more concerned with Amos, addressed himself once more to his friend.

"Amos!" he whispered, as softly as he could, "I'm not supposed to be here — so keep your voice 'way down or we'll both be in terrible trouble. Now," and he clasped his friend's hand, so great was his relief at being able to ease the racking pain of Amos's whip cuts, "tell me what this is all about!"

Amos, feeling entirely recovered, thanks to the properties of the salve, sat up smiling, his eyes sparkling.

"It's like this, Chris. You went, and you didn't come back. I could see that Mr. Wicker was uneasy, and then you came back for a little while. But when you went a second time, that was too much for me! I know what Claggett Chew can do, 'most as well as you do, and nothing he could *ever* do is good! No *sir!* So — I had to get here. But how?"

He paused to draw breath but Chris urged him. "So? Go on!"

202

"So," Amos told him, "I cast around in my mind: how do I get where Chris is, I says to myself, and stay there, to be ready to help him when the time comes? He's all alone, where he is; I don't like that." Amos's face grew long and solemn. "Now Chris, I'm your friend, but to anybody else — outside our family, 'course, Mr. Wicker, Miss Becky and all, or at Riveridge, where everybody's happy too — outside of those two places, what am I? Just a colored boy. I'd be a slave anywhere else. You know that. So —" Amos grinned and punched Chris in the ribs as he stifled his laughter, " — that's what gave me the notion. I'd *be* a slave! And to make it seem for true and for real, a beaten slave doesn't leave ary doubt, now do it? So," Amos swallowed and looked down at his hands, "I had to work hard on Jonah to get him to beat me good." Amos glanced up, and at the sight of Chris's expression, glanced away, shamefaced. "Jonah's a good friend. It hurt him bad as it hurt me, but he understood why he had to do it." Amos looked at his hands again. "Never thought I'd see a big fellow like Jonah cry, but he did, raising up the whip and bringing it down. He cried, tears all down his face, saying, 'That's enough — huh, Amos? Say that's enough?' " Amos wagged his head with a hint of Ned Cilley's refusal in it. "But I made him beat me *good!* Claggett Chew and Simon Gosler can't be fooled," Amos ended, in a whisper.

Chris just sat there, numb, for a long moment, his face incredulous. Then he put his head on his folded arms on the bed and the tears he owed to an unshakable courage and friendship were shed for Amos — "just a colored boy."

CHAPTER 27

*L*OYAL AS HE WAS, Amos's arrival as a runaway slave greatly complicated Chris's situation, rather than easing it. For one thing, Amos was not to know, on Mr. Wicker's instructions to Chris, that Chris could take on shapes other than his own. Nor must he know, out of kindness, that Chris's real century was far ahead. The knowledge of all these things would only have bewildered Amos and made him even more unhappy than he was at Chris's occasional lengthy and unexplained absences. Mr. Wicker thought it best, and Chris agreed, that for Amos, Becky, and his other friends in the eighteenth century, he be simply of their own time. Their sorrow at his departures was keen enough without knowing how far into the future he really went.

So, sitting up at last, wiping his eyes with the back of his hand and snuffling, because he had no handkerchief, Chris looked dolefully at Amos, wondering how his friend could help as he wished so much to do. Amos was looking tactfully away from his friend's tear-stained face, pretending to be unaware that Chris had shed so much as one tear, and was staring, puzzled, at the yellow cat. The cat sat at Amos's feet looking back at him in a friendly way.

When Chris's stifled sobs had stopped, Amos, with his head still turned, commented in a low tone, "That's a most 'straordinary cat, Chris. I've seen many a cat, but this cat looks the way I'd look, was I a cat."

Chris thought to himself that Negro intuition was hard to equal, for without knowing it Amos had solved the riddle of the cat by immediately feeling its humanness. Still, Chris felt that for a while Amos had better be kept in ignorance of who and what the cat was.

"Amos," he said, whispering the words, "you're right, that *is* a special cat. In fact, we have to save that cat and let no harm come to it."

Amos gave a low *humph!* "Save a cat! Law', Chris, a cat's got nine lives, for a start — eight more'n we have. *They* should be looking out for *us*, was there ary justice." He sighed. "People do say as how there isn't justice, leastways, not so much, so I suppose we two-legs an' one-lifes has to look out for four-legs and nine-lives." He reached down to stroke the yellow head. The cat closed its eyes with pleasure and happiness at being noticed, and began to purr. "Anything special we do?" Amos wanted to know, as if anything was possible now that he and Chris were together again to brazen out the danger.

Chris hesitated. "You know how it is, Amos. Danger doesn't ever give much warning — if any. What *is* important is to let no harm come to this cat, and second, *never* let on that you are part of Mr. Wicker's household. If you should ever let *that* out

205

we're gone geese! Claggett Chew's least favorite people are Mr. Wicker and me." He pondered a minute and then added, "There's an old woman here, Mamba. She's very dangerous. She's out to do harm to Agona, and he's someone we need to keep an eye out for too. Then there's a pigmy — Baka; he doesn't seem to have made up his mind which side he's on — Mamba's or Agona's. And there are the two slaves you saw downstairs. They're loyal to Agona."

Amos leaned over to whisper back. "What you mean, 'two' slaves? I've seen and heard, of a whole crowd of people here, not just two — "

Chris took a long breath, sighed again, and poured into Amos's ear the story of the zombies. Amos's eyes grew bigger than ever, his jaw dropped, and he turned several times to stare unbelievingly at Chris, who nodded his head, crossed his heart and drew his finger over his throat, which made his account absolutely true thereafter as far as Amos was concerned. Even so, the Negro boy found it a tall tale to swallow.

"If you say so, Chris, it's so. No salt or they go back to they graves? 'Deed, I don't know which I'd ruther *not*: walk around half dead on the *outside*, or lie down dead as dead on the *inside!*" Amos sat and thought. "But the cat — that's something else yet again. I'll look after him best I can."

"And Amos," Chris urged, "keep your ears and eyes open to see what you can discover?"

Amos's eyes began to shine as they always did at the hint of coming adventure.

"Certainly will! And start now, I guess?" He got up and stretched with as much ease as if he had not a short while before been fainting with pain. "No time like the present, Miss

Becky do say, so — guess I'll see can I make myself useful."

Chris had a last look at his friend's back. "It's remarkable how fast that salve works," he murmured. "Now Amos, remember. Simon Gosler is as shrewd as they come."

Amos nodded his vigorous agreement. "Only one worser, and that's you-know-who!" he whispered back. "Wish me luck and don't *you* get into any kind of a fix!"

Chris's hand and Amos's were held firm in a long clasp, and as they grinned good wishes to one another, Chris felt a lightening of the worry he had carried, alone, in Claggett Chew's house. Extra care though he might be, it was good to have a friend nearby. A moment later Amos, a natural-born actor, went slowly down the stairs, as if every step was a torture. Chris, standing still and holding his breath, heard the miser humpback's pleased growl.

"So? Down to do your share, eh? Very well. Help Agona lift that wet cloth out with the pole, and then hang it over those long rods until some of the dye has run out. So! You show him what you want done, Agona, and see that he works well, or he will not be worth feeding!"

The yellow cat ran out into the attic and Chris followed, thinking over his next move. Standing at the curtained entrance to the room he could, at a moment's notice, disappear into the shape of a fly or a mouse, should Simon Gosler or one of the slaves come up the stairs with a new length of cloth for drying.

Standing there, Chris's heart skipped a beat as Simon Gosler unexpectedly limped over to the stairs to climb up one or two steps and sit down to nurse his peg leg. From there he could oversee the work of the slaves from a more comfortable, and a higher, vantage point. Chris, in his own form, felt far too exposed. One upward glance by Gosler, and he could not fail to be seen. He hesitated a moment more, deciding what shape he should adopt as a safe disguise. He renounced the idea of being a mouse — the mouse was supposedly eaten, and with Claggett Chew one could never be sure. He was apparently away, and yet — The boy took back the form of the black-capped chickadee, hiding under the hanging corner of a fold of drying woolstuff. From there he could see straight down the stairway to where Simon Gosler sat, and as he hunched into the shadow of his hiding place, the miser's words were carried up the stairwell to where the bird perched.

"So — Simon has neither bet-prize of gold nor aught else to hold over Chew for a king's ransom but a cat. A yellow cat!" he whined to himself. "Yet, old Gosler has a trick or two up his sleeve. For is he not now alone and his own master? If the cat should disappear before Chew gets back, how is Simon — attending to his duties so closely and so well, as he always does — how is Simon to know what's become of a yellow cat? Has it wandered? Has it been stolen? Alas, who shall know, once the animal is gone?" He cackled at his idea and at his plan, rubbing his knotty fingers with their ragged dirty nails together in his sour glee. "Simon Gosler knows of a place to hide a cat, and hide it he will!"

The humpback glanced from side to side, as if fearing that a slave could have overheard him. Then, with his lopsided agility, he hopped up from the step to go down and berate Agona and the slaves once more.

Chris, despairing for the yellow cat's future and wondering what to do next, took back after a long wait his own form, and

tiptoed into the drying attic.

He stood looking thoughtfully at the bands of color in and out of which the cat was feinting and skittering in some game of its own. Now it ran under the brown cloth colored from a dye made from walnut shells. Now under a yellow dyed from the inner bark of the hickory tree, and at one side it patted at a thread hanging from the blue worsted dipped in indigo that had been grown in North Carolina. And as the cat came scampering back to bat at a shadow and jump, turning in mid-air before it alighted on all fours and went dashing down the stairs full tilt — as any real cat might do that felt lively — Chris felt a sudden and terrible misgiving.

The cat had behaved so much like a real cat. Could it be that true feline qualities were growing in it, like a dull film over the human character of the child, pent up inside the coat of fur? Was it possible — and Mr. Wicker said that all things were possible — that gradually, perhaps more quickly than he had knowledge of, the cat could become entirely a cat, never more to return to its proper form? Chris went cold at the thought, and tiptoed to a window to see if he could see where Jean-Jacques had gone.

The yellow cat was in the sun of the square. It was stalking a red bird, precisely as a cat *would* stalk a bird, and Chris remembered how the French boy had loved the little feathered creatures. Now, joined with a cat's natural hunting instinct, there was a double incentive for the animal to trail any and every bird.

Chris lazily watched the cardinal-bird hopping ahead, hunting for seeds; the cat creeping behind. Footsteps sounded on the stairs; Chris turned himself into a fly and hid under the bed as the two slaves came up the stairs carrying heavy wet cloth to be stretched out over the drying-rods. Then they moved to other lengths, now dry, to be taken down and folded, and carried down to the long counter below where they were to be wrapped, ready for transportation to the shops of Georgetown.

As he made himself small under the bed in its darkest corner, something nagged at the back of Chris's mind. It was something to do with the bird. It was a cardinal-bird, right enough,

210

but something was wrong; something was missing.

He began, with an increasing feeling of urgency, to search his memory, trying to visualize again the hopping bird and trailing cat.

The slaves, after some time, completed their work and went down the stairs. The sun had gone down, and dusk was spilling like a kettle of overturned indigo over the land and the stream. Chris had just retaken his own shape when Agona came hurrying up the stairs, followed by Amos, both carrying their bowls of food for the evening meal. Agona's eyes searched the room with a rapid glance and then he looked down the darkening length of the attic.

"Where is the cat?" he asked.

"It was outside stalking a red bird — " Chris began, and they all moved to the window overlooking the twilit square.

The cat was not in the square; but far off, at the distant end of the long pasture, something tawny moved, jumped, and disappeared. And already the humpback had glimpsed his quarry far off and nearly lost to him, for he could be seen even then hurrying along the edge of the stream, dragging a sack after him.

Then Chris remembered what was wrong with the cardinal-bird. It was scarlet, a male bird, but it had no crest.

He turned an anguished face to Agona. "Claggett Chew! He's back! That bird — "

Agona did not need to be told. He nodded somberly. "Far up," he said, "there is a cave, and the springs that make Dragon Run. Where the cave leads, far back, no one knows."

Chris wasted few words. "How do I find it?" he asked.

"Follow the stream — that's all I know," Agona answered. "Shall I come with you?"

Chris shook his head. "No. If I don't come back sometime during the night — then — "

"Let me come, Chris!" Amos cried.

Again Chris shook his head. "No Amos. The best way you can help me now is to guard Agona." He looked back at the big man. "Mamba has buried a knife near the *kingolo* bush — there, at the top of the waterfall," he said pointing. "She may mean to use it tonight — on you, Agona."

Agona's mouth spread in a slow smile. "Look!" he said, pointing to a corner of the eaves, low and close above their heads. "See that little square of wood? On that square Agona has painted a picture of Mamba. When it rains, and the rain water flows from the spout, it will wash over the picture, wash and wash, and as the picture is washed away, so too will Mamba's life fade. Even should she kill Agona, she too will not last." The giant lowered his pointing finger and dropped the heavy hand on Chris's shoulder. "Here, boy, eat quickly, then go. They are not too far ahead. You will have to wait for darkness for safety."

Chris knew this to be good advice. He ate rapidly, a little from Amos's bowl and some from Agona's, and as he ate he resolved how best to follow Claggett Chew, Gosler, and the cat.

To be a fish, it would be hard to swim upstream. To be a mouse would take too long, on a mouse's short legs through the heavy grass. To be a fly was truly dangerous, for Claggett Chew as a bird could make one snap at him and his life would be over. To be a bird — Chris remembered only too well how desperate a fight he had once had against Claggett Chew who took a hawk's guise, dropping like a plummet through the air at his prey. There remained one way to go — as himself.

He set down the bowl, looked at the dark beyond the window, and stood up.

"Wish me luck!" he said.

CHAPTER 28

*T*IPTOEING   DOWN the creaking wooden stairs Chris made sure that no one was left in the big dyeing shed. A streak of light shone faintly beyond the door of the wing. The boy eased it open and slid out. The front window of the house was alight. Going noiselessly up and standing on a stone, Chris could just see over the window sill into the room within.

It was Claggett Chew's sitting room, on the other side of the wall from the huge fireplace of the dyeing shed, and Chris remembered vividly how he had watched Simon Gosler hunt for his misplaced coin there so short a time before. The room now was empty, but the briskness of the fire told Chris how recently Simon Gosler had been gone. Nor had he expected to leave, that was evident, for an uncorked bottle and a mug stood on a table near the fire beside a comfortable chair, and Chris guessed that Simon had thought to sit down for a while in peace and comfort. Probably he had glimpsed the cat far down the field, but, without doubt being unaware of Claggett

214

Chew's magical powers, the humpback would have no inkling of who or what it was that the yellow cat was following.

Keeping close to the walls, the boy slid along silently until he could be clear of the building, and any hostile, unsuspected eyes. Peeping in at a window of the shed he saw the slaves, Mamba and Baka, sitting moodily near their fire; the rows of the zombies along the walls staring into their own terrible limbo.

Beyond this part of the buildings Chris was on the trail of Claggett Chew, Simon Gosler and the cat. He decided that the quickest way to cross the stream was to follow Agona's example. Accordingly he jumped to reach the overhanging branch, and hanging from it with both hands, found it by no means as simple to shift across the stream as it had seemed for Agona. His arms felt wrenched from their sockets, but he succeeded, dropping gratefully to the farther bank.

The black line of willows growing along the opposite side of the stream cast the irregular shadows of their branches across the water to make a crisscross of pattern on the bank. In and out of this dappled protection thrown by starlight and the moon, Chris ran. He soon reached the end of the pasture, and there Dragon Run branched off to the left. Thickets massed themselves impassably among the willows on both banks; Chris changed himself to a trout, swimming hard against the current as he moved past the impenetrable interlacing twigs.

Gradually the bushes thinned and the stream ran through a natural grassy space. Seeing a sandy slope near the edge of the water, Chris changed back to his own shape. Searching the sand he saw a series of indentations in the soft bank, and examining them by the gray light of the rising moon he found

them to be paw prints and boot marks. Simon Gosler and
Jean-Jacques, at any rate, were then not too far ahead!

Chris straightened up, and as he did so he heard a low heavy
rumbling noise. With misgivings, the boy ran across bright
moonlight patches between shade and shade, until, clinging to
the round black column offered by the bole of an elm tree, he
found himself on the brink of a melon-shaped pool. Trees
were spaced around two sides. The third side, near where he
stood, opened its low rock wall for the outflowing of the

stream. The fourth side, facing Chris, was a cliff of stone, rising like a fortress above the clear water. And where a few minutes before there had been the entrance to a cave, there was now only a heap of large boulders. Dust was blowing airily away from the great stones, and Chris realized that the only way into the cave had been blocked but a moment before.

The moon, indifferent and remote, sent pointed white fingers probing through the branches of the trees into the clear water in front of the boy. So intense was the light as the moon sailed, unclouded, over the night sky, that it even called out a hint of green from the mossy stones that lined the pool. The moonlight showed a wavery bubbling where a spring gushed from the earth, a dark trembling force coming from immediately below the entrance to the cave.

It gave Chris an idea. Nothing ventured, nothing have, he thought, and saying over the magic words to himself, with a deep breath and a dive that took all his strength, as a trout once more he made straight for the bubbling spring.

It needed every ounce of both courage and muscle, for Chris had no way of knowing whether he would come up inside the cave, or be forced back. Or — a nightmare thought — trapped within the narrowness of the spring and drowned, fish though he might seem.

Fighting as any speckled trout against water current, the fish slowly forced its silvery way past the mossy boulders, over the clean sandy floor of the inner spring. All was blackness and rushing, shouldering water, yet still the fish persisted. Its lungs began to hurt and its eyes felt as though they would start from their sockets. The fish, fighting too the pounding pressure in its head, knew it had only seconds left of vitality, when a spinning gleam broke the total dark. A last terrible second of effort, and the fish had forced its way to the base of a stony waterfall and the top of an interior pool, and gasping, drew in mouthfuls of air and spray as it rested, panting.

Looking about at last, Chris's fish-eyes saw that he had won his way into the interior of a cave. A swinging light flecked the high walls of the cavern. Quickly Chris changed to his own shape and pulled himself up the rocks near the narrow waterfall to see where the light came from.

As he peered cautiously over the perpendicular crags he could see a familiar bareheaded figure. In one hand Claggett Chew held his whip. In the other he held a sack with something round and squirming inside. And facing him, enraged and panic-stricken, stood Simon Gosler holding a lantern.

CHAPTER 29

HE HUMPBACK, standing sideways to Chris's view, faced his captain and his partner with turbulent emotions plainly showing in his face. His long years of association with the evil pirate, their voyages under sail from one end of the earth to the other and back again, many times over, had given Simon Gosler ample opportunity to study every vengeful or fitful mood in Chew's twisted nature. Now Chris, peering with infinite caution from behind a rocky outcropping — for the spring lay five feet or more below the floor of the cave — found himself a scant distance from the two men. He changed himself into a fly with the speed that is spurred by fear, and crept into a crack in the stone. From there he could see everything before him but be hidden, even from Claggett Chew, with a fair degree of safety. Pressing himself tightly back into the welcome crevice, Chris gave all his attention to what was being said.

Simon Gosler was struggling with a difficult decision. The cat — the king — he had intended to steal for himself and hold as the pirate's, if not a nation's, ransom money, was still a cat in a bag. And that bag had been wrested from him and was in the hand of the man standing so much too still before him. Chris could see that the miser was torn by his own avarice and obsession for gold, and by a well-founded fear of Claggett Chew.

As Chris looked and listened, Simon's fear got the better of him, or else he thought that to swallow his anger would, for a time at least, soothe his master, who, he knew very well, would stick at no wrongdoing or evil deed. Chris saw the convulsive working of the hunchback's throat, literally choking back his rage at losing the prize he had felt so certain of being able to hide; and deadly fright at finding himself in a cavern that had no known way out, now that the entrance had been blocked by the fall of rocks.

The lantern he held shifted and swung in his shaking hand. Its light shafted dimly in the vastness of the cave, and at last Simon Gosler tore his gaze from the unblinking eyes of the pirate to glance, terror-struck, about him.

The cavern was high, its arched vault lost in deep shadow. To the right, a hundred feet away, a black opening to what seemed a passage could be seen, leading into complete obscurity. Looking to the left, Chris followed the direction of the miser's eyes. He could see on that side the great boulders that had been tumbled down to wall what had been, perhaps, only a small half-hidden entrance into the large cave beyond. Dust still sifted and trembled on the air, teasing the nostrils toward a sneeze. Simon Gosler's clothes were marked by the dry sides of the rocks he had brushed against as he had scrambled into the cave in pursuit of the cat, and to hide it there. Chris, eying the pile of stones, reasoned that there must have been one stone

220

larger than the rest which Claggett Chew had loosened, closing in an instant, with rocks of all sizes, the way out to the fields and the moonlit pool.

His sly eyes flicking from side to side, unable to be quiet under the stare of the silent pirate, Simon Gosler wet his lips with an uneasy tongue, and attempted a crooked smile that held no mirth. Even so, he had to clear his throat a time or two against the bitterness of his rage and bafflement, and to down the fear that was so obviously invading him, even as the cold of the underground was creeping up from the soles of his feet to his knees and his whole body.

"Eh! Eh! Cap'n, what is the meaning of tumbling them rocks a-down behind us, eh?" He set the lantern down, and out of long habit began rubbing his bony fingers, weaving them together like the legs of two embattled spiders, in his gesture of servility and false humbleness. "Sure, I never seen you! All I saw was our precious cat, a-hoppin' after some bird. I thought to save it, for no telling how far it might not have wandered —" He gave a shifty look at his master to see how well his remarks were being received. Claggett Chew's face remained expressionless, his eyes coldly watchful under the jutting black brows. The miser's eyes slid away and he began again, his tone taking on an increasing whining sound, pleading and wheedling. And indeed, Chris wondered if, in spite of his years of service to Claggett Chew, he might not at that moment be in danger of his life. Chris, little liking though he had for the humpback, quaked at the thought that a violent deed might at any moment be done before his eyes.

"So — heh! heh!" the cringing man went on, "you have him safe." The narrow distrustful eyes slewed toward Chew's face

222

and away, like lizards over stones. "And how do we — leave, good cap'n, eh? Heh! Heh! 'Tis a dark place, here. Do you lead on. I'll follow, as the good cap'n knows Gosler has done, and faithfully, these many years — "

The man hesitated, stumbled in his speech, and stopped. A silence fell, rippled only by the delicate crystalline fall of running water. His fly-eyes, with their many facets, enabling him to see both Simon Gosler and Claggett Chew at once, Chris could see the cold perspiration start out on the forehead of the miser, catching an oily upward gleam from the lantern at his feet. The humpback began to shiver uncontrollably, for the continued silence of the pirate, the silence of the vast underground room, and the steady stare from eyes Simon knew had witnessed the murder of many another man, would have combined to unnerve stronger men than he.

His shivering grew until the miser's teeth chattered in his head and he was shaken as by the ague. The cold of the dark place made itself increasingly felt, and Claggett Chew, still standing stiffly wordless in front of him, staring and staring, became at last too much for the humpback. His hands clenched at his sides, he gradually raised them as he lifted his contorted face to the remorseless man.

"Is this how I am to be repaid after all these years, eh cap'n? Do you mean to leave me here to die, in this icy chamber, as payment for many a dreadful deed Simon did for you, that you were careless of doing for yourself? Eh? *Eh?*"

His voice rose fairly to scream the final words, and still Claggett Chew said nothing, nor did he move. This immobility roused Simon Gosler even more, but now to depths of fear he had not touched before. Moving shakily forward, his

223

legs barely able to hold him upright, he snatched with his claw-like hands at his pirate master's coat, twisting the cloth in his agony, and gazing up into the blank face of his tormentor.

"You wouldn't do Gosler in, cap'n, now would you? Come now, well you know I am your good right hand, to do your bidding at any time, day or night, as I always have? Spare Simon, cap'n, sir! Don't leave a pore ol' humpback in this hidden place — why, none could hear my cries if you should leave me!"

He stepped back to smooth frantically at the creases he had made in the lapels of Chew's coat, his fawning voice a travesty of what it usually was, and the sweat of fear running down from under his hair to blind his eyes and make him blink and squint. His hands, unwashed and as repulsive as the man himself, tried to pat soothingly at the jacket of his relentless master, but only succeeded in making nervous jabs.

"What has pore Simon done to displease his noble captain? Speak, good cap'n, gracious cap'n, best of all masters! Tell pore Simon where his fault may lie, that he can undo whatever harm there is, and be once more within his captain's grace."

The mean, covetous face cocked itself to one side in as coaxing a way as it could muster, the restless hands folded and unfolded themselves in a series of prayerful claspings that, each time done, Simon would undo, as if still resisting an abject appeal to the pirate. In the blinking orange light of the lantern, Claggett Chew's voice finally pierced the echoes of the cave as a spear is flung at a fleeing prey.

"You false sniveling toad! You dirty ingrate! Do you still, after all these years, know me so little that you fancy I cannot read your simple little ratlike mind?"

224

He took a sudden stride forward and Simon Gosler took as sudden a one back. To Chris, the fact that Claggett Chew's face showed no emotion of any kind made it even more frightening to see than if the big man had been in a towering rage. As it was, his cold set face, his deep harsh voice, nearly without inflection to relieve its paralyzing tone, affected the boy as no other man ever had, and, he felt sure, never would again. He wished with all his heart that the scene would come to an end, and that some means, now hidden from him, would appear whereby he could rescue poor Jean-Jacques, pent up in the sack that dangled from the pirate's hand.

"Did your restricted cockroach brain imagine that I, Claggett Chew," thundered out the terrible voice, "was not aware that you intended stealing this prize?"

He swung the sack high aloft, and a small frightened *miaow* came floating down like a feather of sound to Chris's straining ears. Claggett Chew strode again to lean forbiddingly over the cringing form of Simon Gosler, who, in a panic of terror, shrank back, his knees buckling under him.

"I left you alone today on purpose, you cheating ninny!" the pirate went on, "and overheard your mutterings. 'Yet, old Gosler has a trick or two up his sleeve. For is he not now alone and his own master?' " mimicked the pirate, with a nasal exaggeration that made Simon's face go whiter than it already was. "Never mind where I was to hear you — I heard, as you see," sneered Chew, straightening up to look with scorn at the shuddering miser. "But your words were not needed. I know you too well, false humpback!" So saying, Claggett Chew, with one hand, ripped the coat from Simon Gosler's back, and the false hump with it, to throw it down with distaste and disdain at its owner's feet. "Such a treasure as the one I hold was one you would never be able to resist, and well I knew it!" He spat his disgust into the very face of the miser. "Did you really think to get the better of Chew, who has never yet been bested?"

For a flashing second a ray of life shot into Gosler's eyes as he slid a look upward.

"Never bested — are you sure, master?" he sniffed, his hands working again. "I am the last one to know of them all, that's sure, but if I wished to tell — "

Claggett Chew's cold rage rose, at this phrase, even greater than before. Chris realized that Gosler referred to the two occasions when Mr. Wicker's magic, combined with his own skill, had all but finished the pirate. They were incidents Chew probably did his utmost to forget, and hid from all men's knowledge save that of Simon Gosler, who alone remained of his villainous band.

"Ah!" cried the pirate. "So ye'd taunt me? Eh, by me soul, I have had enough of you and your falsity and of your greed!" and whistling out his whip he made to slash Simon across the face or the eyes with it.

The wretched man threw up his arms to ward off the blow, and his scream of terror sent echoes in their turn screeching over and over from wall to wall of the cave. Simon Gosler sank to his knees and then fell prostrate before the man with the whip, wailing and begging.

"No, no, good master! Spare Simon, who meant you, by my blood and bones, no harm! Indeed, spare me, and I'll work as never before! Let me live, good cap'n, noble man, prince of pirates! Spare poor ol' Simon and you'll never regret it, on my

226

heart and soul and on my head!"

The raised hand with the whip, tipped at its metallic end with a fatal poison, was slowly lowered, and Claggett Chew stood pondering above the groveling miser, who wept and in his fear beat at the ground with his fists.

"On your head, you say?" muttered the pirate. "Well, so be it. One move from you, however lightly false, and you are a dead man, d'ye hear?" he snarled down at the snuffling creature in the dust.

"I hear!" wailed Simon, still not daring to look up. " I hear, oh heaven bless my noble captain!" He sobbed in thankful relief now, after the strain of his long torment.

Claggett Chew stepped back, revulsion at the abasement of the man before him evident in his face.

"Thank the Devil and you'd do better, dust-eating worm!"

He strode to the cave wall near the entrance to the tunnel that led into pitch-blackness. When he returned, the watching boy could see that he held a pick. This he flung at Simon Gosler, who reached out his clawing fingers to grip it with the desperation of a man not yet secure from death.

"See how good I am to you, worthless grub!" growled Claggett Chew. "Dig your way out, if you can. There is the means. Follow me, and you will surely die, for no man, not even you, who knew this cave, knows its recesses and its turning as do I." He put a hand into a pocket to draw out a small object which he threw on the ground near Simon Gosler. It was a candle stub, no longer than Chris's thumb.

"And see, I am humane, I leave you light to dig by, valueless mole! But you will have to work fast, for the candle will not last you long! As for the lantern," said Claggett Chew, "*that* is for *me*."

So saying, he swept up the lantern from beside the kneeling miser and made off with his powerful strides toward the black passageway to the right, while Simon Gosler, fearful, hopeful, and revengeful all together, scratched wildly at his tinderbox to light the candle before he should be left alone in the dark.

228

CHAPTER 30

*C*HRIS WAS FACED with as delicate and difficult a decision as he was ever to have to take. In what guise could he safely follow Claggett Chew? The pirate-magician's acutely sensitive intuition would make any form unsafe. Chris remained rigid, seeing the lantern light swinging toward the tunnel. Nearby, Simon Gosler lit the candle stub and began with all his strength to dig at the stones in an effort to free himself, but not without a long look over his shoulder at the disappearing figure of his master.

The light, far down the vaulted passage leading farther into the cavern, was waning. An arched glow the color of cumquats showed the height of the high natural walls, but with every step Claggett Chew was drawing farther and farther away, and with him went Jean-Jacques. Chris, as the rocking light of the lantern shrank like a withering fruit, felt that some decision had to be made. He chose what seemed to him the most natural disguise, and one in which Claggett Chew might just possibly be unaware of the real identity within, though this was a re-

mote hope: Chris chose to be a dog. The frantic miser's back
was to him; muttering and groaning, Simon's attention was on
the rock wall that lay between him and freedom.

A minute later, just as the last residue of light faded completely, a smooth-haired dog, very much a mongrel, with a
white body spotted with large black and russet blots and two
black lopped-over ears, shook itself as it stood at the top of the
craggy drop. It gave a last backward glance to the way it had
come, then, hurrying, it loped forward, putting its nose down
from time to time in the hope that its dog-qualities could catch
a faint scent of Claggett Chew's boots, or the smell of cat.

Chris tried to keep a sense of direction, and it seemed to him
that the caves opening one out of the other and leading down in
a gradual slope, were doubling back to follow the line of
Dragon Run.

That makes sense, Chris thought to himself. At one time —
how many thousands of years ago! — there was probably an

underground river here, which finally ground out these caves from the limestone. The stream, Dragon Run, is all that is left of it. Perhaps a sudden hot flow of lava, when the world was made, embedded the river. Anyway, it does seem to be turning to the right, and going back the way I came.

Running with its nose to the ground, a smell of smoke and roasting meat came to the dog long before its eyes saw the wash of light up over the walls ahead. Silently, and with enormous care, it crept forward.

Peeping around a projection of rock, with scarcely more showing than the wet tip of its nose, what a sight lay before Chris's astounded eyes!

Claggett Chew had chosen to stop in another vast cavern. But what made Chris's eyes spread were the paintings on the cave walls. Deer, cattle, a bear, a herd of bison were portrayed with master strokes upon the stone. They seemed as alive as if done that selfsame day instead of perhaps twenty-five thousand years before.

Glory! thought Chris, prehistoric hunters! They had to know how to do that, for once they put the animal-grease and ground stone color on the walls — and that's what I've heard they used — then it was there to stay. Every stroke had to be right, and right it was! He looked from one painting to the next. There's a cow jumping over a fence, he said to himself, so they knew how to catch them, even then. And there are buffalo running! Glancing away to the man near the fire, he surmised: and Claggett Chew knows the place well — he never even gives them a look; he's used to them.

The brigand was engrossed in searing a strip of meat before the flames. Chris, noticing the direction of the blowing smoke

231

took heart, for a faint draft pulled the smoke ahead out of sight into the dark recesses of the cave beyond. The sack Claggett Chew had carried only twitched and heaved infrequently. Chew paid it no attention, and began eating the burned meat, speared on the end of his knife, tearing morsels off with his teeth. He drew a leather flagon from his capacious coat pocket and took alternate bites of meat and pulls at the bottle.

Good, thought Chris. At this rate he'll fall asleep. For a while, anyway.

Sure enough, it was not long before Claggett Chew leaned back on the dry sand of the floor, with his boots toward the hot coals, and appeared to drop off to sleep. The firelight flickered up the cathedral curve of the walls, its movement seeming to give motion to the leaping animals so superbly depicted. Chris did not need its help to imagine that once again these prehistoric creatures were racing and springing on the plains overhead, where they had strayed when the world was young.

Looking and imagining, the boy waited, watching the fire die and deeper shadows fill the spaces of the cave.

How to get the cat? As far as Chris could see, a cord bound the neck of the sack. He was debating whether, as a dog, he could drag the bag far enough away from Chew to be able to safely open it, when he saw pointed white teeth pierce the sacking, aided by a pair of rending claws. A second more and the large furry head of the yellow cat poked out from the sack and shot a glance at the sleeping man.

Chris judged the time safe; in any case it was a chance he had to take. Rapidly taking his own shape he made signs to attract Jean-Jacques's attention. The cat saw him and redoubled

232

its efforts to get free. Chris pointed and gestured to the black
caverns ahead and the cat nodded. Chris was about to change
to his dog-form when he had a flash of inspiration. He did not
know if he had the power to take the shape he wished, for he
knew that even the magic taught him by Mr. Wicker had its
limits and he could not take all or any form. This one was so
good that the boy made every effort of will and concentration
to achieve it, standing in the slow red of the distant fire, saying
over to himself the magic formula.

Just as Jean-Jacques squeezed and wriggled out, dashing away down the inky passage beyond, a second yellow cat, as alike to the first as two eyes in one head, ran forward to join it.

Pride, they say, comes before a fall, and so it proved. For in the exuberance of his new disguise Chris leaped impertinently over the face of the dozing Chew. The breeze of his motion awakened the sleeping pirate who reached out with incredible speed almost as if he had never been asleep at all, and caught the second yellow cat — Chris himself — by the tail. With a wrench that seemed to pull every muscle in his body askew, Chris tore free from the angry man, and with the deadly sound of the whistling whip in his ears, rushed with the speed of fright and danger after his double. The way ahead was as dark as if the cats were blind, and behind them as they ran they could hear the nearing curses and drumming feet of the infuriated Chew, drawing closer as they dashed forward into blackness.

CHAPTER 31

*HRIS, HIS CAT-EYES* and knowledge adjusting themselves to the dark, knew that at any moment Claggett Chew could change himself into another shape the better to gain upon the two fugitives. Running hard, and hearing the muffled *hush! hush!* of Jean-Jacques's catpaws beside him, Chris took breath, slowed, and listened. Claggett Chew's heavy boots were not to be heard. Puzzled for a moment, Chris decided that the pirate must have gone back for his lantern.

This gave both Chris and Jean-Jacques time to plan, however hastily, and look about them. Taking back his own shape, standing in pitch-black, Chris dared to put his fingers into the bag of magic odds and ends. What he expected he did not know. That something to help them both was in desperate need was evident, and he reached into the little bag with speed and hope.

He drew out something roughly oval. Not being able to see what lay in his hand, Chris could only guess. It felt like a closed mussel or oyster shell. Somewhat daunted at how he

235

was to use this, Chris felt for the close-joined edges and pried them open.

Instantly a penetrating sheen spread far ahead of the two opened halves, and Chris and the yellow cat, blinking, looked in to discover that the glow came from a large pearl, shining inside the empty shell. Looking around him, Chris saw that the magic of the light was such that no reflection showed behind them to give away their whereabouts. This seems to have some of the properties of infra-red rays, Chris thought to himself, but there was no time to consider what sort of magic he held. The important thing was that he held it. Moving forward again down the long arched tunnel where they were, Chris could feel air being pulled past him and knew they were headed toward some faraway exit.

"Jean-Jacques," he whispered, "let me carry you, for no telling how long we may have to wander. And — if we come to branching directions, you take one way while I let Claggett Chew see me and follow down the other. Then you can come back and trail *us* if he gets too close for comfort."

When the cat began to shake its head, objecting to too much danger to Chris, Chris simply grinned at the anxious eyes and scooped the warm furry body up under one arm. Holding the shining oyster shell in his right hand he started forward once more at a steady trot.

The tunnel, or ancient riverbed, that they were following, seemed to Chris to be going parallel to the way he had come. Once he stopped and listened for Claggett Chew and in the utter silence he could faintly hear the rustling sound, deadened by distance, of water running over stones. Chris felt hopeful, for he took it that this must be Dragon Run, somewhere not too far above them.

Soon the cellar-like stone walls bent sharply to the right, and Chris remembered where the stream had branched, where the thickets had been too tightly interwoven to admit him. His heart began to lift, and putting down the yellow cat, they ran forward with increasing confidence.

There was no warning, no sound. A growl and yap reverberated to the roof of stone overhead, lost in centuries of darkness. Staccato noises rolled and echoed as a dog of tremendous size sped along the tunnel behind them. Both knew that their fanged pursuer was no dog but Claggett Chew, bent on the recapture of Jean-Jacques and perhaps Chris's death, which he had been cheated of so often.

Without knowing how it happened Chris and the cat were running as they had never run before, and as they ran Chris knew he must change back to his yellow-cat shape, in order to confuse Claggett Chew as to which was the real Jean-Jacques.

Running, straining, once more he put his fingers into the magic bag.

He pulled out what looked like a seed pod, such as he had often seen on fences in the fall, those filled with white, silky, densely packed milkweed seeds, each seed with its white parachute to drift it to a new rooting place. Having no time to decide on how to use it, Chris, his ears stunned by the barking and baying of the monstrous dog leaping so close behind them, threw the open seed pod over his shoulder.

A second later, at the snapping and snarling that immediately followed his gesture, Chris ventured to look around.

238

The seeds were not the ones he knew, white and umbrella-shaped, but silk fibers which blew out in every direction as they fell, interlocking themselves like a nylon spider web of unbelievable toughness and resilience. A barrier of milky innocent-looking threads formed a misty net from wall to wall, against which Claggett Chew, first as the dog and then as himself, battered and hacked. How long this resistance would hold — not so much against Claggett Chew as against his virulent magic — Chris could not know, and at a bend in the cavern where he was hidden from view, he took on the form of the yellow cat. Jean-Jacques stared at his double with astonishment and then a hint of amusement in his enormous eyes.

On they ran, having to trust to instinct, since Chris had prudently slipped the oyster shell back into the bag before changing into the yellow cat.

Only too soon they heard the challenging shouts of success, and as they reached a second vast rocky hall, heard the pounding of the pirate's boots resounding on the cavern floor.

A quick glance in the faint light shed by his enemy's approaching lantern showed Chris that from this new stone chamber two ways branched out. One bore slightly to the left; the other straight ahead. The mock yellow cat motioned with its head to the left-hand way; Jean-Jacques at once, though with a backward look, vanished into the blackness of this narrower, smaller passage, while Chris resolutely waited, poised for flight at the mouth of the cavern ahead.

He stood lashing his tail in anger as a cat would, and it took all his courage to wait for the pirate, for well he knew how Claggett Chew enjoyed dipping the wire tip of his leather whip in a deadly poison, and he did not doubt that the violent man

240

had done so before starting after him. The jumping light of the lantern bobbed and ducked from side to side of the walls he had just run past as if it too wished to escape, and Chris gritted his teeth to force himself to stand, waiting for his old enemy to catch sight of him.

Claggett Chew came pounding into view, his evil deep-set eyes seeming to send out a shine of their own as he saw what he thought was his lost cat. With a last flirt of its tail the cat whirled and ran nimbly forward, Claggett Chew close behind.

But as he faced about and began running once more, the lantern light behind him showed Chris something that made his heart nearly stop with a new terror.

The limestone floor of the cavern into which he had to run was deeply pitted with large holes. They were large enough to swallow up a man's body, let alone a cat's, and there could be no knowing how far down they went. Or, Chris conjectured as he desperately ran, whether they had a bottom at all.

CHAPTER 32

*I*F CLAGGETT CHEW held his lantern, and Chris watched carefully and was exceedingly spry, he felt he might escape the tremendous limestone pits. Not knowing exactly where he was headed — something, he suspected, that Claggett Chew did — the boy had no idea how far he had to go before he might be able to escape from his terrible predicament. Even as he leaped, dodged, and ran, tiring and panting, he wondered if the pirate would once more change his shape. He decided that the evil man would remain himself, for taking another form would mean losing the use of his whip and his lantern, both invaluable to him at that moment.

Ahead of him he saw still another pair of cavernous openings. Now he was baffled on which way to run and blindly chose the one to the left. Whisking around a jut of rock he changed himself in desperate haste to a bird that soared back high over the oncoming pirate's head.

Quick as he was, Claggett Chew was his match, for as he passed over the pirate's upturned face, back the way he had come, the leather whip whistled up, barely missing him, and the curses of the villainous man echoed below him, ricocheting from wall to wall in a basketwork of stuttering sounds.

Darting back, now in almost complete dark, to where the caves had doubled on themselves, Chris flew into the one on the right, his eyes wide in the blackness. He followed the freshening feel of the air. As soon as he dared, he came gently down, fanning hard with his wings and seeking ground under his feet. Down and down he went, but to his reaching feet came only air. He kept dropping slowly, until with a start of horror he realized that he was sinking into one of the deep limestone pits. When he was about to fly up again light moved above his head, and looking up, he could see the foreshortened figure of the pirate standing over the very pit where he fanned the air despairingly, tiring fast.

Chew looked all about, and muttering curses went back, still hunting for Chris. The lantern shine went with him. At last the bird rose, laboring with its wings, to the top of the pit, where it sank exhausted on the rim.

He knew he must not stay there long. He must find the way out, and then with Agona return to find Jean-Jacques. Listening as hard as he could, he could hear Claggett Chew stamping far away in the vast stone chamber through which they had both come. Chris uneasily retook his own shape, opening the shells of the pearl for light.

As he moved the sheen around him to get his bearings, he saw to his consternation that this was as far as he could go: there was no tunnel, there was no outlet. And yet — there was the draft of air. Picking his way between the scattered pits and holding the shell close to the walls, the boy noticed that the

ceiling of this natural room was far lower than had been any
of the others. It was nearly circular, and he could easily imagine how water had swirled around during hundreds of years
to make this smooth-walled place, perhaps dropping at last
through the holes it had made in the stone floor to some lost
underground river that, for all anyone knew, might still be
flowing its mysterious way under the earth to the sea.

The pearl-light caught pockmarks of shadow on the surface
of the wall, and looking closer Chris saw that the marks were
shallow toe holds cut from the rock. The boy lost no time.
Holding the shell between his teeth so that both hands would
be free, he began climbing rapidly, wondering where he would
come out.

He rose from the cavern into a narrow, warm place. As his

head came to the top of the stone barrier, a faint luminescence showed above and he smelled wood smoke. His head rose into space, and Chris found to his stupefaction that he was within the fireplace in the dyeing wing, to the right, beside the swinging dye kettle. And although he had felt that he had been underground for half a lifetime, it was still night. No glimmer of moonshine showed beyond the window that he could just glimpse around the curved black iron pot.

Then for the first time he became aware of the patter and drip of rain. Far overhead the boy heard it drumming on the roof of the attic and gushing from the rainspouts of the building. The fire immediately below him was low, covered over with ashes to keep it alive for the morning, and the boy, relieved at his safety, was on the point of struggling over the stone wall that appeared to be only a shelf at the side of the fireplace, when a movement nearby held his attention.

It was Mamba. Mumbling and crooning to herself near the hearth, she looked to Chris to be strangely older, and more brittle than ever. She was moving her hands in a rhythmic motion, looking down at the hearthside.

Chris craned his neck. Two figures lay supine on the floor. They were Amos and Agona; Mamba had hypnotized them into a trance. Their eyes were open, but, like the zombies, they were without energy or will. Mamba's face was triumphant. She moved one old veined hand before the face of first Amos, then Agona. Neither blinked nor moved.

She bent slowly, never taking her eyes from her victims. When she straightened up, she held a familiar odious bowl in her hands — it was the skull-bowl of death that held the broth of the *kingolo*.

"Open your mouths and stretch forth your hands!" commanded Mamba, and like automatons Amos and Agona stretched out their hands and opened their mouths for the deathlike liquid.

"Drink! Drink deep!" ordered Mamba, and put the bowl first into Amos's hands.

It was then that Chris leaped.

CHAPTER 33

*O*NE VAULT, AND Chris had jumped clear, his shoes slapping squarely into the heaped ashes, scattering red-hot embers in every direction. Mamba, holding the repulsive skull toward the outstretched hands of Amos, was so taken by surprise at this unforeseen interruption that her own mouth dropped open in amazement as her head came up at the noise. With one swift swing of his hand Chris knocked the skull upward. His only intention had been to keep the drink from Amos, but his anger and his aim were better than he had bargained for. The skull, with its deadly contents, flew straight up into Mamba's face, and the full force of the liquid was dashed into her mouth and down her throat. Her reaction, for she was still shocked by the rapidity of Chris's action, was simple and human: she swallowed.

The *kingolo* broth dripped from her face and the empty skull rolled grotesquely away across the floor. And as Chris stood facing the wicked old woman, her face changed gradually before him. The light of understanding faded from her

248

small winking eyes. They glazed as if death itself crept over them; her body sagged, her head rolled. She who had sent so many into her own form of death-in-life had been made into a zombie.

Chris shuddered and turned away, sickened. Outside, the rain poured down, and abruptly to Chris's nostrils was borne the acrid smell of burning cloth. He looked, liberated from the eerie spell of Mamba's transformation, to see that the hot embers his feet had scattered had done their work. As he glanced up, a ragged flame soared, catching at now a piece of sacking, now a heap of wool, now a bolt of folded cloth. Before Chris could blink the wing was in flames.

There was not a second to lose. Chris turned, horror-stricken, to his friends. They were still as inactive as before, and Mamba's influence to free them from their trance was lost forever, imprisoned as she was within her own spell.

Chris, the flames crackling behind him, chafed the hands of his inert friends. No response. He slapped their cheeks. Not a flicker of true life. Once again the boy, nearly crying with anxiety, put his fingers into the magic bag.

All they drew out was a small red berry, like a single red bead from a holly bush. Chris eyed it for a moment, and then its pungent smell tickled his nose and he sneezed. Smiling, he held it quickly to the noses of first Amos and then Agona. Each, at the strong heady smell, took an involuntary deep breath, sneezed, and woke to reality with a start and a questioning look.

The flames were roaring up the wooden staircase close beside them. The only way out was the door near the front of the main house.

"Quick! Amos — Agona! Out — out!"

Their bewilderment was still so strong that Chris had to take the hand of each and lead them toward the door.

Gold, scarlet, and white-hot, the flames ate everything in their path, twisting around the timbers with pointed greedy fingers. A great beam crashed behind them; the door, when Chris pulled it open, added a stormy draft to the growing inferno inside.

"Out! Out!" was all he could shout above the roar and hiss of the fire.

Agona suddenly became himself again, and swept both Chris and Amos under both powerful arms as if they weighed nothing, to run from the wing as the floor of the attic, with all its lengths of colored cloth, crashed with an upsurge of flame and sparks to the floor they had left only a minute before.

Standing in the lashing rain, Chris, water flattening his hair and soaking his clothes, cried out, "Mamba! What became of Mamba?"

Agona shook his head. "She has gone to join the evil ones who live in fire. Had not fire consumed her, the rainwater would have washed her to nothingness. She was old and evil. Fire and water are both clean. In the end," said Agona thoughtfully, "Mamba was made clean."

Chris shivered. "What about Simon Gosler? Did he get back?" he asked.

Agona nodded and pointed to where, through the smoke and fire, the humpback could be seen on the far side of the burning shed, darting at the flames as if to save a bit of cloth here and there.

"I think only the wing will burn," said Agona, "for see, the

250

rain pouring off the roof is putting out the fire near the rest of the house."

So it seemed, for already the side of the house where the majestic fieldstone chimney rose, was sputtering and hissing as the fire died, while the rest of the wing shot spears and arrows of flame against the silvery battalions of the rain.

"Agona! We have to find the yellow cat!" Chris urged. "Claggett Chew is there — in the caves — he chased us both! Too long to tell now, but we have to get back — and fast!"

Agona bent his head in agreement. "Amos," he said, "go tell your real master what we do. And tell my sister Abby, that Agona, King of the warriors of Watusi, has knowledge of where she is and shall find her." He looked down at Chris. "I have a message for Baka, and an order for the zombies. Then we go to find the yellow cat."

Chris waited while Agona went inside the slave shed, while Amos, still groggy from his hypnotism, started back to Riveridge.

The wing where wool-stuffs had been dyed was now only a few charred standing timbers and a mass of sizzling burning wood, before which stood Simon Gosler, wringing his hands, unaware of Chris and Agona, who had moved around near the stream.

Agona rejoined Chris, and by the lurid trembling glow of the funeral pyre of a priestess of Erzilie-Gé-Rouge, the big man and the boy shifted hand-over-hand along the willow branch above the waters of Dragon Run.

Dropping to the far bank the giant Negro stripped off his shirt, found the hidden rope under the bank, and pulled. Chris admired the red play of fire on the night-dark skin, but looked

252

with a weakening of the knees as the scarlet polish on the water's surface broke into a circle the size of a cup, and the water was sucked below. The circle grew, the water hummed and sang, and at last gave a shout as it plunged underground. Chris stared down at the black pouring stream, striped with the red glare from the fire, as if Dragon Run was taking a part of the sparks and flame into the earth with it on its strange and secret journey.

"Jump!" commanded Agona, who possessed a new quality, almost an added height. "I follow!"

Chris did not want to be thought a coward, but he had been through a great deal that day. He hesitated, peeled off his coat, and looked at Agona. The face above his was implacable and stern.

"Jump!" cried the giant again.

The black water glistened, and dived at terrifying speed into the unknown channel almost straight down.

"Dive or I push!" shouted Agona fiercely.

Chris took a deep breath, said a prayer, and plunged.

CHAPTER 34

*T*O *CHRIS'S HAPPY* surprise the engulfing water tunnel was, after the first second's dive, far from frightening. Quite the contrary, he found it as exhilarating as sliding down a water chute into a pool. The water was too cold for comfort, true, but there was not, as he had imagined, any feeling of being stifled. The underground tunnel proved to be big enough for even so large a man as Agona, which left plenty of space for Chris. There was, it appeared, little water beneath him; enough to form, over the smooth limestone mossy with damp, a slippery surface that shot him downward.

Around curves he went in a deep twilight but not total darkness. His arms still out ahead of him in diving position, Chris was just beginning to enjoy the extraordinary coasting sensation when the stream rushed him into a dim chamber. There the boy thought it proper to scramble out and wait for Agona.

Wringing his clothes as dry as he could, he found that he had lost one shoe somewhere; presumably it had sailed on ahead of him. He kicked off the other, wrung out his stockings, and looked about him.

He found himself in a hall unlike any of the caves through which he and the yellow cat had run a short time before. For a moment Chris had a confused impression that he was in a wood of moss-boled trees, for all around were tall columns going from floor to ceiling, of an underwater green. The effect was dreamlike. From beyond Chris's right shoulder, far ahead, flowed a pale light. It touched the dense forest of columns, drawing from them peacock-feather blues and greens; an emerald mist that deepened into strong sapphire shadows.

Wonderingly, Chris stared, and it came to him what this strange wood was. It was a cavern of stalactites, hanging from the roof of the cave. Stone had been formed from slowly dripping water over countless thousands of years. The water brought a film of lime with each drop, so that by minute degrees a stone icicle was made. But these columns were whole. That meant that they had been joined to their doubles, rising up from the floor of the cave: stalagmites. One dropping from the ceiling, one rising from the floor, long, long ago they had gradually fused. The damp air of the cave had encouraged the moss, and so the whole cave had come to have the atmosphere of some lost forest growing underground.

Chris turned to look back the way he had come for Agona. Agona should have slid to meet him some time before, but there was no sight of him, and a waiting silence seemed to hang within the green stony glades around him. The boy looked at the runnel of water flowing in the stone trough along the south wall of the cavern, and as he gazed pensively at it, before his eyes it thinned, slackened, and trailed away

255

to nothing, leaving only mossy damp.

Chris was tired. Where he was he could not be sure, and the sight of the dwindling water could mean only one thing: Agona had had to close the trap above so that Dragon Run could flow on as before. For some reason he was detained from joining Chris.

Fatigue and despair settled like a swarm of gnats over the lad. He shivered, swung his arms to warm himself, and turned, disheartened, away. How to look for Jean-Jacques? Where to start? His feet in their wool stockings made no noise as he moved over the mossy floor. Suddenly, almost upon him, through the closely ranked green columns he glimpsed a mas-

sive white shape. Alarmed, moving from cluster to cluster of the stone trees, Chris warily drew nearer.

The green boles stopped halfway across the cavern, and along the far wall was a sight Chris could not credit. He shut his eyes, opened them again and pinched himself, but the unbelievable remained there for him to see.

A tremendous white dragon lay along the whole side of the thirty-foot length of the cave, its terrible head laid sideways on its forefeet, its back crenelated like a castle's walls, and the stretch of its tail lost in the weedy depths of the cave. Chris's heart skipped a beat; holding the mossy side of a stalactite, he shook his head. Real it was, but no longer alive. The great dragon of Dragon Run had come into its cave a final time, thousands of years before, to die, and the lime water slowly dripping had turned its prehistoric body to stone.

This, then, was Agona's discovery! This the Cave of the Dragon where the yellow cat would be safe from all harm! And as Chris stood staring at the green-white outline in the uncertain light, as if he could never look enough on such a fabulous spectacle, a sharp sound, as of a heavy heel on stone, broke the silence.

Alert at once, Chris retreated hastily into dimmer recesses of the underground wood, for the blanched light of dawn was growing beyond the mouth of the cavern, enough to cast a faint shadow from his body to break the symmetrical design of the stone columns.

Flattening himself behind a group of three stalagmites and looking from side to side so that he should not be taken by surprise from some unexpected quarter, Chris saw a streak of apricot yellow weave at a blurred speed between the trunks of the stone trees.

The yellow cat! Chris was on the point of rushing out, when a snarling curse split the air, and Claggett Chew emerged from the back of the cave that was lost in obscurity, to run, sliding on the slippery floor, after his quarry.

"You are mine!" he spat out in his rage. "A nation's ransom, for so I heard it from your own lips, and so you are! More money than I could ever spend — whether I sell you to the Royalists or the Revolutionaries of France!" His harsh voice reverberated coldly from wall to wall like the crack of his sinister whip.

The cat at his words underwent a curious change. From

a terrified animal it took on an air of resolve and anger such as Chris had never seen it display before. As the hidden boy looked on, the yellow cat raced toward the back of the cave, leaping high into the air at one point, as if jumping over some obstacle that to Chris was invisible.

Claggett Chew swung about, his whip whistling out to entangle the cat's legs and bring it down. The cat dashed behind a green column and peered out, hissing, its back arched. Claggett Chew was in a towering rage at being for so long balked of his prize. In front of Chris's eyes the pirate became the great dog he had been before, chasing around the columns as he tore after the cat.

The cat was still too agile for him. It ran up the stone back of the dragon, and when the dog saw that it could not reach it, the dog became a hawk, swooping up to pluck the cat from its refuge. Spitting its fury but still seemingly unafraid, the cat leaped into the air directly at the oncoming hawk, scratching at its eyes and inflicting some well-aimed damage, for the hawk gave a cry and blood-stained feathers floated to the ground. Claggett Chew tried a last change of form. The hawk became a leopard, matching with its own limber springs and speed the gallant efforts made by the cat. The cat was tiring, valiant though it was. Chris, shocked out of his amazement, pulled the magic rope from about his waist.

With sure gestures the rope flew in and out, and before the leopard — occupied by the dodging cat — could notice what had occurred, a rope elephant lumbered out from behind a protecting group of stone pillars. With Chris directing what was to be done from where he sat behind the rope ears, the powerful magic elephant seized the leopard around its belly with its rope trunk and was about to dash its head against the white stone sides of the dragon.

A scream rent the air of the cave, not the scream of a leopard, but the scream of a man facing imminent death. Still in the implacable curl and grip of the rope elephant's trunk, the leopard became a twisting, struggling man. With his one free hand that held his whip he lashed up at the boy on the elephant's back. The boy ducked; the mighty trunk of the magic beast threw the pirate's body along the floor of the cave. Claggett Chew slid, unable to stop himself, and from his higher position Chris could see where he was headed. Behind Claggett Chew lay what the yellow cat had jumped over — a moss-grown, limestone pit.

With a shriek so terrible that Chris put his hands over his ears to stifle it, Claggett Chew, struggling to stop but not able to, skidded into the pit and disappeared. His screech, echoing and whirling, grew fainter and fainter as he fell downward into black space.

CHAPTER 35

*T*HE *MAGIC ROPE* elephant had done its work, and it was a matter of seconds for Chris to jump down, turn the elephant into just a rope to wind about his waist, and catch up the trembling yellow cat. Then he ran for the luminous opening of the cave.

The roar of water became louder as Chris and the cat advanced. Soon the green mists of the dragon's cave were left behind and they stood back of the largest of all the waterfalls, beyond the house, near the bridge.

Chris wasted no time. That Claggett Chew was gone he did not trust, although it would seem, even for a magician-pirate, impossible to win his way from the apparently bottomless pit into which he had fallen. Looking on all sides, the boy spied footholds in the perpendicular bank. Too steep to get down, it was perhaps possible to climb up. Binding the cat safely to him with the magic rope, Chris grasped the wet slippery rock and made his way up carefully, away from the cave of the dragon. The boy and the cat came slowly over the bank's top into the rays of the sun slanting over the Blue Ridge hills.

When they reached the top of the bank a frightening spectacle lay before them. Simon Gosler was hitching up his wagon and team with desperate haste, as toward him from the door of the slave's shed marched the zombies, armed with knives, gnarled clubs, scythes and stones. On they came, straight at the frenzied humpback, who, buckling the straps of the harness and glancing fearfully over his shoulder at the steadily advancing horde, was shouting orders to which the zombies, deaf and sightless, gave no heed. Just before the first of the mob reached the miser he managed to jump to his seat, grasp the reins, and shouting at the horses, drive at a gallop toward the road. He stood up in the wagon, whipping up the nervous steeds with panicky gestures.

He was not quite in time, for the zombies threw their stones and clubs after him, and duck though he would, Simon Gosler's ugly head and falsely humped shoulders received many a hard hit to hurt and bruise. He vanished down the road in the direction of Vestal's Landing in a rising cloud of steam from the laboring horses.

Chris glanced at the house. It already looked abandoned. The door hung ajar, and final wisps of smoke from the burnt-out wing rose falteringly on the early morning air. As he got to his feet, setting the yellow cat gently down on the grass, Baka came from the shed to send a long low call into the growing sunlight.

The zombies stopped, obeying, and Baka drew near them holding a bowl. He dipped his forefinger in the bowl, and then touched one by one the mouths of every zombie. Chris

263

knew that at long last these poor sufferers were being given,
on Agona's orders, the grain of salt that meant eternal rest.
As each zombie tasted the salt, a last life came to their bodies,
which moved with unaccustomed vitality. With a start, each
looked wildly around, and then, as Agona came from the shed
in new robes of red and orange, lemon, purple and blue, impressive with a majesty that left no doubt as to who he was,
the zombies ran in all directions. Back they fled to their graves,
hidden some near, some far, in unnoticed places. Agona, regal

and brilliant in the sunlight, watched them go with satisfaction and compassion in his face.

Chris felt a great weariness enveloping him. A gray blanket seemed to be muffling his head and dulling a part of the polish from the rising sun's light on the trees. Agona, followed by a quiet humble Baka, the two loyal slaves and the young Negress, came to him with deliberate steps across the strawed autumn grass. At Agona's approach the yellow cat put up its furry face on which there seemed almost a human smile, and

265

opened its pink mouth in a *miaow* of greeting.

"Now is the time," Agona said in his deep voice, and Chris saw that the two slaves once more held a white dove and the ritual bowl, while in the young Negress's hands was a dish of wheat flour. "The evil ones are gone," Agona pursued. "In this new sun, let me liberate the boy. Here is a smooth place for the pattern of sacred flour; for the offering, and the dove."

Once again the Vodun rite was carried out, but this time it was in the sparkle of sun that danced on the chanting water, with Agona in his flowing robes of prism colors, scarlet, azure, chrome. There was no longer the terror of the first night. Gone was all fear. Instead, a rising spring of relief and happiness bubbled up like the transparent waters of the spring where Dragon Run had its birth, its fresh clarity running over the emerald rocks in a distant pool, serene in its crescent of trees. Chris understood now that nothing and no one could taint Dragon Run. It renewed itself from deep hidden places, unseen and undiscovered, and in spite of all that had been frightening and sad in this house, the water running, running, made all new, endlessly.

He experienced a wonderful lightness of heart as he stood watching Agona draw the mystic patterns on the ground, the wheat flour sifting back to the earth from which it had been taken, from between the strong dark fingers of an African king. A king to free a king; that was how it should be, Chris thought. That was how it could only be.

Agona called upon Damballa-Oueddo for the power to liberate a boy from the skin of a yellow cat. The bowl of blood was poured onto the ground, the blood of the white dove was touched to the forehead of the patient animal sitting with

266

its tail curled around it on the morning grass.

As Chris watched, so exhausted that he felt neither asleep nor awake, the cat began to shake before his eyes, to smear and become distorted as if Chris saw it through a misshapen piece of glass. The cat-head vanished, blending into the face of a lively little boy with square-cut hair. The furry body and striped paws, the paler belly and long tail were no more. Jean-Jacques, king and son of a king, stood under Agona's heavy dark hand, looking with trust and thankfulness into the face of the warrior king of the Watusis, African tribe of Ruanda-Urundi.

Agona got up slowly, his work done, and the small hand of a boy went up for comfort into the big warm fingers.

"Take running water and wash away these marks," Agona said to the two slaves and the Negress. "Wash them well, that no trace remains, for there is no place in this land for the rites of Voodoo. For this land is fresh and new, and will not make its peace with the somber rites of unhappy wanderers from a ravaged land."

The clear water flung over the ground left only twinkling flashes on the blades of grass.

"Come," said Agona. "Perhaps at the big house there will be work we can do, and a new home."

As they reached the avenue leading to Riveridge, a tired, odd assortment of people, the sun streamed over the mountains and fell upon a neat figure dressed in black, waiting for them halfway down the drive as if he had known all along that they were on the way.

CHAPTER 36

*B*ACK IN MR. Wicker's sitting room in Georgetown, Chris and the magician sat in their accustomed places in the two red leather chairs before a good fire. Their feet stretched to the flames, Chris was still sniffing from a mild cold he had caught in the dragon's cave, but the familiar sitting room was cozy. Beyond the red brocade curtains snow was falling, heavy flakes making plump woolly lines along Mr. Wicker's espaliered fruit trees in the garden, and hooding the box shrubs with puffy white nightcaps. Chris, peaceful, broke the silence.

"It certainly feels good to be home, sir! Nice as Mrs. Moffit is, and Riveridge is a beautiful house — still — there's no place like home, is there?"

Mr. Wicker was meditative as he looked into the fire. "No — so they say, my boy," he said, and fell silent again.

"I'm glad Mrs. Moffit forgave Agona for scaring her," Chris went on. "I would never have guessed he — or any man — could have walked on stilts over fifteen feet high." He nodded

to himself. "And as for dancing on them to prove it to us —
if he hadn't done it before us all I should never have believed
it!"

"An extraordinary sight," Mr. Wicker observed. "Putting
carved wooden panther-paws on the base of the stilts was very
ingenious. Very ingenious indeed! I do not doubt," said the
handsome quiet man, "that in Africa this threw any followers
off the track — "

" — while they thought they were on it!" Chris could not
resist saying. Mr. Wicker smiled.

"Quite so, Christopher. While they fancied they were on
it. Here, of course, as you and I both knew, a panther-print
was decidedly out of place."

"Yes sir," Chris agreed, wrapped in his own remembrances.
"I think Agona will be a wonderful overseer for Mrs. Moffit,
don't you, sir?"

Mr. Wicker nodded absently. "He is a leader born, and a
remarkable man. Quite evidently respected by all Mrs. Moffit's
workers."

"Why wouldn't Aunt Abby talk to you, that first day, Mr.
Wicker?" Chris asked. "Did she know her brother, Agona,
was Claggett Chew's slave?"

Mr. Wicker considered, his head bent and his fingertips together. The firelight edged his black clothes and smooth head
with its own tender touch.

"Yes and no, my boy," he said. "I do not think she had ever
seen him — Certainly he had never seen her, for he did not
know she was so close by. Although perhaps he had heard
that she was in the vicinity. No, Aunt Abby may have caught
a distant glimpse of Agona in the fields. Family ties are strong.

Perhaps something stirred in her memory. They were separated when she was a child, so he said, and he was younger than she." Mr. Wicker's voice, the voice of a highly intelligent and civilized man, added another kind of warmth and richness to the room.

"Why both children were not taken from the African coast with the other slaves is not clear," he went on. "Agona was then perhaps too small, he was only three or four, and their mother was ill, or so Aunt Abby told me." Mr. Wicker sighed. "I expect the slave traders decided that Aunt Abby was stronger and more likely to survive the journey."

It was Chris's turn to sigh. "What a thing, sir! All those people, of all ages, huddled in the holds of small ships!"

And he remembered the song Baka had begun and the other slaves had taken up.

Over what seas did the slave ships sail?
Toward what sun, toward what moon?
Under what stars did our captors sail?
On what sad sea that we never saw?
Tell us, how shall we find our home?

The melancholy air, as it flowed back into his mind, seemed to bring a cold shadow into the cheerful room and recalled too vividly and too closely, the terrors he had experienced at the house on Dragon Run. Mr. Wicker sensed the sadness in his pupil and brought a gayer note to the conversation.

"Well, my boy, they are all well cared for now, at Riveridge. Mrs. Moffit paid handsomely for every one of them, for Ned Cilley delivered the sum to old Gosler this morning."

271

Chris sat up. "He's about, sir? What about Claggett Chew?"

Mr. Wicker shook his head. "Gosler is about, right enough, and probably up to no good, as usual. Claggett Chew has *not* been seen."

Chris shivered. "Do you think — ?"

Mr. Wicker brooded, understanding the question. "I do not know, Christopher. I do not trust the man. He *may* be gone for good. I wish — uncharitable as it is to say it — that I thought he was. But one apparently can never be sure."

"What about Jean-Jacques, sir?" Chris wanted to know. "He was well hidden in Mrs. Moffit's coach all the way back, so that Simon Gosler should never hear of him." He smiled. "He seems as happy as a lark with Becky Boozer, and she is having such a good time, fattening him up! Will he stay here, do you think, sir?"

Mr. Wicker rose to pace the room with his hands behind his back. At last he said, looking out at the snow and the pewter sky, "No, Christopher. That would not be wise. He would not be safe." He paused, as if unwilling to go on, but at last he did. "The *Mirabelle* is to dock tomorrow, and within a few days I shall take the boy on board myself. He must be got away."

Chris turned, uneasy, in his chair. "Where do you propose to hide him, sir?"

Mr. Wicker was silent for a time as the firelight grimaced at the snow beyond the windowpane.

"I shall take him far off, Christopher, to a newly opened settlement. It is in Canada, in the Hudson Bay country, a large tract of land under the management of the Earl of Selkirk, and called Selkirk's Settlements. The Earl's wife is there with him;

272

she is a kind woman and will care for Jean-Jacques. He can grow up in peace, that far away, and it will come to pass that what he learns from the Indians there and his own observation of birds and animals in those forests will be the basis of his career. A career," said Mr. Wicker carefully, "that will become a part of America's history and pride." He turned his back to the snow to face Chris. "Remember that when you get back, Christopher. Look in the fine books available in your time, and see what our little friend made of his life. He will capture birds on paper as no one else ever has," said the magician, and at Chris's puzzled face he smiled briefly. "I forgot to tell you his last name, did I not, my boy?" The profound eyes lighted for a passing moment. "The last name is Audubon," said Mr. Wicker.

Chris had scarcely paid attention to the final words. He got up, his forehead creased.

"What did you say, sir? 'When I get back'? Do I have to go already?"

Mr. Wicker smiled, a sad musing smile. " 'Already?' My boy — you have been in the eighteenth century a long while. Yes, I am afraid it is time for you to return."

"Oh, sir — " Chris began, and swallowed, because he knew it was no use, once the moment had come for him to go back. He hung his head and scuffed at the carpet with the toe of his new shoe. "Could I just have a glimpse of Becky and Amos, and Jean-Jacques?" he asked, in a whisper.

"Just a *glimpse*," said Mr. Wicker firmly.

The time that he could stay with his friends in the past never seemed to last, and now that Chris stood in the shadow of the corridor looking into the big familiar room redolent of good food and friendship, it seemed no more than a flash since he had come back for the longed-for visit.

Hard as it was to bear, Chris felt that it would be less of a wrench for him, and for those friends he loved and whom he knew loved him, if he did not talk with them again. His heart ached at the inevitable parting, and it was all he could do to keep himself from rushing into the kitchen.

Looking in now, with Mr. Wicker standing slim and tall behind him, the rosy bloom of the kitchen fire blossomed in

reflection in Becky Boozer's cheeks, only to be echoed again and again in the twenty-four roses nodding cozily among the twelve waving black plumes on her outrageous hat. She was at her usual task, getting together "a little something" to keep Jean-Jacques from being seized with hunger in the night.

At the table in front of the Water Street windows, although now the curtains were drawn so that Jean-Jacques should not be seen by Simon Gosler's wicked eyes, bushy-browed Ned Cilley sat with his knife and fork bolt upright in his two fists, wearing his habitual expression of happy anticipation that fought with the attitude he tried — hopelessly — to adopt, that his "stummick was peevish today." Next to him sat Amos, cheerful in being at home once more, and beyond him still, the young French boy. Jean-Jacques's eyes were wide at the unaccustomed sight of Miss Becky Boozer, for which no one could blame him. His round eyes followed the vast buxom woman as she bustled competently about. And they opened wider still as she came to the table with the first of her "morsels."

"Sure now, me poor boy," she exclaimed, setting down a meat pasty and a bowl of hot soup, "you've had a worritsome time, so the good master has told me, and you're that peaked-like! You seem like a bird!"

"I should like that, Madame Boozair," piped up Jean-Jacques, smiling at the kindly face above him, and giving a side glance only, out of restraint and politeness, at Miss Boozer's irremovable bonnet.

"Hark at him!" Becky addressed Amos and Ned. "He would like to be a bird! Nay, young man, let Becky fatten you up a bit first, so that you'll have some strength to your young wings." Up went Becky's broad hands to her broader hips. " 'Madame' says he!" she muttered, quite flustered as she moved back for another assortment of dainties. "Fancy the French knowing so much, scarce out of the cradle! La! Tck! Tck!" Becky clucked, pretending to be scandalized at such precocious manners and secretly delighted.

"Here now!" she cried. "Eat a wee taste, or every man Jack of you will wake in the night with such a rolling in the belly from emptiness — fie! 'Twill be a pure scandal! And me here to cook for you? Try to savor a smidgin, Ned Cilley, it will settle your stummick, so it will. Try these pickles, or a bit of cheese — or — here, plum tart and cream; me own preserves, so they are! Or a sliver of the beef roast — 'tis good for growing boys, Amos. Or apricot fool, light as a feather — ye'll scarce know ye ate it!"

So urging, coaxing, cajoling first one and then the other, Becky Boozer stood by anxiously, uneasy that her delicious dishes might go untasted. As Chris knew only too well, this

276

had never yet been proved to be the case, and on this occasion the table was once more covered to its last inch with every kind of food tempting to the appetites of any man of any age. All three at the table fell to with a good will that brought a smile at last to Miss Boozer's merry face.

"There now!" she cried, better satisfied. "Sure, ye'll sleep well this night, every one of you!"

Before she could turn around and perhaps catch sight of him, Mr. Wicker's long forefinger touched Chris's shoulder, and with the picture in his eyes of his friends in the candle glow and the firelight, with snow swaddling all noise from the quiet world he had to leave, Chris turned away.

In the sitting room, he knew, he would leave his eighteenth-century clothes and put back those of his own time. He would stand, as he had now twice before, on the hearth before Mr. Wicker. His friend and teacher would blot out from his mind with a drift of his hand, the knowledge of magic that had to remain in the century he loved.

He was ready all too soon. The red curtains, the figured Indian carpet, the shining silver of the pitcher on the table had never looked gayer or more inviting. But Chris knew better than to try to prolong the time. He looked up at Mr. Wicker, no longer so far above the level of his eyes as he had been the first time they had met, years before.

"I'm ready, sir," he said. He swallowed hard. "You know how much I hate to go. No need to say, either, that I want to come back — "

"So, my boy," said the man in neat black, not really replying, "as you said earlier, 'There's no place like home.' Come. I shall go with you to the door."

CHAPTER 37

*W*E WERE JUST DISCUS-
sing, Chris," his father said
as the boy came slowly in
his own front door, "that
little house with the waterfalls." He gave his son a sharp glance.
"What's the matter with you?" he inquired mildly. "You look
as if you'd lost your best friend — "

"No, sir — that is, I hope not," Chris answered. "I *did* sort
of lose something, I guess you might say — "

Chris's father looked at his wife and raised his eyebrows in
silent query. She shook her head at him. No, she had no idea
of what was on their boy's mind. Commander Mason went on.

"Somehow, that house and the stream stick in our minds.
We'd like to take another look — maybe buy it. What do you
think?"

The transformation in his son's face was so great that Chris's
parents sat up in their chairs, concerned. Chris was beaming
from ear to ear.

"Oh, *could* we, do you think?" he asked, his eyes shining.
"There's caves all around — I want to investigate them! Have

we any books on prehistoric paintings — and what sort of animals lived in those times? Any — kind of — dragons? And buffaloes? And cows?"

Chris's mother smiled. "Hold on, darling! We thought of doing over the *house* — not living in a cave! I didn't know you liked it that well."

Chris moved away toward the staircase and put his hand in his pocket.

"I think we all would," he said. "It's plenty big enough — I mean, it's *probably* plenty big enough inside," and he looked down at his palm to see what his fingers had fished out of his pocket. It was a white pointed tooth. A leopard tooth. Chris grinned, and looked out of the window as he moved into the hall.

"What are you looking so puzzled about?" his father called after him.

Chris replied, but his voice was abstracted.

"What did he say?" his father asked. Chris's mother took up her mending.

"It sounded like 'Seems funny not to see the snow,'" she said, shrugging her shoulders. "I declare, I never have an inkling of what's going on in that boy's mind! Now it's prehistoric paintings!" She threaded a needle. "Where do you suppose he got that cold?" she said, largely to herself. "It's come on him very quickly — "

Chris's father was working on a set of figures on a scrap of paper and his answer was absent-minded.

"Got his feet wet, I suppose. He always does — "

He looked up then, thoughtful, and listening intently.

"Listen!" he said, holding up his hand. "Do you hear that

279

song? Now where could he have heard *that?* Hear that strange tune? One might think it was a Negro spiritual, only not quite — "

Chris went upstairs, turning the leopard tooth that had once been braided in the hair of a friend, over and over in his fingers. Without knowing it he was softly singing:

"Toward what sun, toward what moon?
Under what stars did our captors sail?
On what sad sea that we never saw?
Tell me — how shall I find my home?"

BIBLIOGRAPHY

AUDUBON, Lucy Bakewell (ed.). *The Life and Journals of John James Audubon* (New York:Putnam, 1896).

BACH, Marcus Louis. *Strange Altars* (New York:Bobbs-Merrill, 1952).

BURNEY, James. *History of the Buccaneers of America*, from the 1816 edition (London:Allen & Unwin, 1950).

CARRINGTON, Hereward, and Fodor, Nandor. *Haunted People* (New York:Dutton, 1951).

ESQUEMELING, John. *The Buccaneers of America*, from the 1684 edition (London:Allen & Unwin, 1951).

GOSSE, Philip. *The History of Piracy* (New York:Longmans, Green, 1932).

HUGHES, Pennethorne. *Witchcraft* (London:Longmans, Green, 1952).

JUNGE, Werner. *Bolahun* (New York:Putnam, 1952).

LEIGH-FERMOR, Patrick. *The Traveller's Tree:A Journey Through the Caribbean* (London:Murray, 1950).

LEWIS, Matthew Gregory. *Journal of a West India Proprietor* (Boston:Houghton Mifflin, 1929).

MICHELET, Jules. *Satanism and Witchcraft:A Study in Medieval Superstition* (New York:Citadel Press, 1939).

PEATTIE, Donald Culross. *Singing in the Wilderness:A Salute to John James Audubon* (New York:Putnam, 1935).

ROGERS, Woodes. *A Cruising Voyage Around the World*, reprint from the 1712 edition (London:Cassell, n. d.).

ST. JOHN, Sir Spenser. *Hayti:or The Black Republic* (London:Smith, Elder, 1889).

SEABROOK, William Buehler. *The Magic Island* (New York: Harcourt Brace, 1929).

——. *Witchcraft: Its Power in the World Today* (New York: Harcourt Brace, 1940).

SUMMERS, Montague. *The Physical Phenomena of Mysticism* (New York: Barnes and Noble, 1950).

THOBY-MARCELIN, Philippe and Pierre. *Canapé-Vert* (New York: Farrar and Rinehart, 1944).

TYLER, Alice Jaynes. *I Who Should Command All* (New Haven, Conn.: Framamat Publishing Co., 1937).

NEIDER, Charles (ed.). *Great Shipwrecks and Castaways* (New York: Harper, 1952).

WOODBURY, George. *The Great Days of Piracy in the West Indies* (New York: Norton, 1951).

About the Author

Dr. Lionel Tiger is the Charles Darwin professor of anthropology at Rutgers University and the author of nine books, including *The Imperial Animal* (with Robin Fox), *Optimism: The Biology of Hope*, *The Pursuit of Pleasure*, and *Men in Groups*. He was Research Director of the H. F. Guggenheim Foundation for twelve years, has been a consultant to the Director of Net Assessment in the Office of the Secretary of Defense in Washington, D.C., and is on the Scientific Advisory Committee of the American Wine Institute. He lives in New York City.